"It's mid_____
softly. "_____

Amanda felt her throat tighten with unaccountable tears. "Happy Christmas," she said in a husky voice. She felt as if she had never understood the real meaning of Christmas before now, looking out into the starlit snow with Blair beside her, their breath hanging in frozen clouds. The urge to lean against him was so strong that she forced herself to turn away...and stopped dead as she noticed the mistletoe hanging from the doorway for the first time.

Following her gaze, Blair glanced up at the mistletoe dangling above his head. Their eyes met in the frosty air. "Happy Christmas, Blair," she murmured, and pressed her mouth to his in a kiss that was warm and long and achingly sweet.

Jessica Hart had a haphazard career before she
began writing to finance a degree in history. Her
experience ranged from waitress, theater production
assistant and Outback cook to newsdesk secretary,
expedition assistant and English teacher, and she has
worked in countries as different as France and Indonesia,
Australia and Cameroon. She now lives in the north of
England, where her hobbies are limited to eating and
drinking and traveling when she can, preferably to places
where she'll find good food or desert or tropical rain.

Books by Jessica Hart

HARLEQUIN ROMANCE®
3511—BIRTHDAY BRIDE
3544—TEMPORARY ENGAGEMENT

Kissing Santa
Jessica Hart

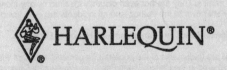

TORONTO • NEW YORK • LONDON
AMSTERDAM • PARIS • SYDNEY • HAMBURG
STOCKHOLM • ATHENS • TOKYO • MILAN • MADRID
PRAGUE • WARSAW • BUDAPEST • AUCKLAND

ISBN 0-373-03581-0

KISSING SANTA

First North American Publication 1999.

Copyright © 1996 by Jessica Hart.

This edition published by arrangement with Harlequin Books S.A.

® and TM are trademarks of the publisher. Trademarks indicated with
® are registered in the United States Patent and Trademark Office, the
Canadian Trade Marks Office and in other countries.

Visit us at www.romance.net

Printed in U.S.A.

CHAPTER ONE

AMANDA saw Blair McAllister as soon as she stepped down off the train. He was standing under a banner wishing everyone season's greetings on behalf of the station staff, but he didn't look exactly filled with Christmas spirit. Instead, he was watching the passengers piling out of the standard-class carriages, his hands thrust into corduroy trousers with barely concealed impatience and dark brows drawn together over a formidable-looking nose.

Dropping her case onto the platform, Amanda slid *A Far Horizon* surreptitiously out of her bag so that she could squint down at the photograph on the back of the dust-jacket. Yes, it was definitely the same man.

With a distinct sense of disappointment, she rested her sherry-coloured eyes on Blair McAllister as he searched the milling crowds with a frown. The photograph had been taken in a desert. Unaware of the camera, he had been smiling at someone out of sight, eyes narrowed against the glare and dark hair slightly ruffled by a hot wind, and he had looked rangy and relaxed and utterly competent.

On the train, Amanda had studied the photograph with interest and a faint stirring of anticipation. She wouldn't have called him exactly handsome, but there was definitely *something* about him, she had decided. She wasn't sure whether it was that look of lean self-containment, his reputation as an intrepid traveller and programme maker, or simply his tan, but, whatever it was, it gave him an indefinably glamorous air.

Now she slid the book back into her bag with a faint sigh. Who said the camera never lied? The man waiting for her on the platform might have the same severe features as the man

5

in the photograph, but in the flesh he looked tired and bad-tempered and not in the least bit glamorous.

He stood quite still, letting the crowds surge past him, and as Amanda watched he turned his head and looked up the platform towards her. For a brief moment his gaze rested on her vibrant figure with a hard, impersonal scrutiny before it swept on, and the next moment he had transferred his attention back down the platform once more. Amanda was left feeling rather piqued at his lack of interest. She was also a little disconcerted by the shrewd intelligence in his face. Blair McAllister didn't look like a man who would be easily fooled by anyone.

Which was unfortunate, in the circumstances.

Amanda hesitated. In London it had seemed so easy to take Sue's place but now, as she faced the reality of her new employer, suddenly it didn't seem *quite* such a good idea. She looked doubtfully along the platform at Blair, then squared her shoulders and bent to tip her suitcase back onto its wheels. She had just spent over eleven hours on trains and she wasn't going to turn round and go back now!

Trundling the suitcase behind her, she made her way towards him through the last of the passengers. 'Mr McAllister?'

He swung round at the sound of his name, the fierce brows shooting up in surprise at her appearing from the direction of the first-class carriages. 'Yes—'

He stopped as he took in Amanda's appearance. She had a mobile expression, and dark, glossy brown hair cleverly highlighted with gold swung around her face. Subject to belated qualms about what she was letting herself in for, she had bolstered her confidence by making up with care on the train, emphasising the unusual golden-brown eyes and outlining the curving mouth with the bold red lipstick that she always wore. She was wearing the suit that she had bought to celebrate promotion to executive status at last, together with her favourite shoes which were decorated with floppy bows and which always made her feel good.

'*You're* Susan Haywood?' Blair went on in disbelief.

Perhaps she didn't look much like a nanny, Amanda realised as his eyes rested for an incredulous moment on her shoes. Nannies probably didn't travel first class either, but Norris had bought her ticket and she had never been one to turn down the chance of a bit of luxury. Still, it was too late to worry about that now. She gave Blair McAllister her best smile instead.

'That's me,' she said mendaciously. 'But I prefer to be called Amanda,' she added, having decided that she would get confused if she had to answer to Sue all month.

'Amanda?' Her guileless smile didn't seem to be having much effect on Blair. Instead of smiling back as any other man would have done, the surprise in his face deepened to suspicion. '*Amanda?*' he said again, staring at her.

'Yes.' She allowed her innocent look to fade in her turn into bewilderment. 'Didn't the agency tell you?'

'No, they didn't.' Blair's voice was terse, with only a hint of a Scottish intonation.

Close to, he was much more formidable than he had seemed at first sight. That photograph had been definitely misleading, Amanda decided. Who would have thought that that cool, uncompromising mouth could relax into such a smile?

Not that there was any sign of a smile now. There was a flintiness about him, a reserve edged with irritability that made him appear dauntingly stern, and although the artificial light made it impossible to tell what colour his eyes were it showed enough to tell her that they held an uncomfortably acute expression. The photograph hadn't warned her about that either, thought Amanda, obscurely resentful. She felt she would have been better prepared if she had known just how they could look through you.

'All the agency told me was that you were an experienced

nanny,' Blair was saying, still frowning suspiciously. 'They assured me that you were a nice, quiet girl.' The penetrating gaze swept from her face to her shoes and then back again. 'You don't look very quiet to me.' His tone implied that he didn't think she looked very nice either. 'You'll forgive me if I seem a little taken aback,' he went on in an arid voice. 'I thought I was getting a sensible nanny called Susan and instead I get a glamorous executive type called Amanda!'

Amanda would normally have been delighted to be described as a glamorous executive, but the caustic note in Blair's voice made it clear that it wasn't intended as a compliment, and anyway, she was still bridling at the idea of not being considered nice.

'I'm sorry if you don't approve of the way I look,' she said in a voice that was intended to sound quelling but which came out more peevish than anything. 'But frankly, I don't see what difference it makes what I look like or what I call myself. I would have thought that the important thing as far as you were concerned was whether I was as sensible as the agency promised.'

'Quite,' said Blair acidly. 'And in my book a sensible girl wouldn't come to the Highlands in shoes like that in the middle of winter, nor would she be travelling first class. If you're expecting me to reimburse your travel expenses, you can think again!'

Amanda had opened her mouth to ask whether he always acted like Scrooge or whether it was just in honour of the season when it occurred to her that getting into an argument with her new employer within the first two minutes of meeting him was probably not the best way of ensuring that she got into Dundinnie. She had staked her career on doing just that, so she mustn't blow it now.

'I don't usually travel first class,' she assured him instead in a conciliatory voice. That at least had the advantage of being true! 'I bought a standard ticket, but by an extraordinary coincidence I met my godfather in the buffet car,' she went on, abandoning truth in favour of improvisation. 'We hadn't seen each other for ages, so he insisted that I go and sit with him in first class, and he paid the difference...a sort of Christmas present.'

'Very generous godfather,' commented Blair dourly.

Amanda beamed at him, pleased with her story. 'Oh, he is.'

'Quite a coincidence meeting him on the same train!'

'Wasn't it?' she agreed, all wide-eyed innocence. 'He got off in Glasgow,' she added, sensing disbelief, and anxious to make sure that he didn't ask her to produce a godfather to substantiate her story.

'Hmm.' Blair favoured her with a hard stare, but to Amanda's relief he didn't pursue the matter, merely grunting sceptically as he picked up her case. 'Well, since you're here at last, Susan, Amanda or whatever you want to call yourself, we may as well go. I've been hanging around here quite long enough.'

Anyone would think that it was *her* fault that the train had been late, Amanda grumbled to herself, but she swallowed her resentment. She had got over the first hurdle, but she would have to be careful. For a nasty moment there she had wondered if Blair had been going to say that he hadn't believed a word of her story, and there would have been nothing to stop him simply leaving her to catch the first train back to London, making an ignominious end to her glorious new career.

Eyeing the straight back ahead of her, Amanda reminded herself just what was at stake. This was her chance to break out of the secretarial rank at last. Norris Jeffries had more or less guaranteed a promotion if she got this right, and if she was going to do *that* she should be thinking about chatting Blair up, not arguing with him.

She hurried to catch up. 'I've just been reading your book,' she said brightly, but the look Blair cast down at her was not exactly encouraging.

'Which one?'

Amanda's mind went hideously blank as she tried to remember the title. 'It was about the expedition you led to the
desert...and you made a documentary when you were there,'
she added helpfully, although she had done little more than
read the blurb on the cover and flick through the photographs.
Travel books had never appealed to her; fiction, the more im-
plausible the better, was much more her style.

'That cuts the possibilities down to about four,' said Blair
drily. 'You don't remember the name of the desert, I suppose?'

'No,' Amanda had to admit. 'But I thought it was terribly
good,' she made haste to console him. 'Honestly, it was great.'

'I'm glad it made such an impression on you.' There was
no mistaking the acerbic note in his voice this time and
Amanda bit her lip, feeling rather silly. Anyone else would
have been glad of a compliment, she thought, instead of making it clear that they didn't believe that she had read a word
of his book! She had been going to pretend that she had seen
some of his television programmes too, but she wouldn't
bother now!

Outside the station it was dark and cold and gusts of rain
splattered against her face. Unprepared for the sharp drop in
temperature, Amanda screwed up her face and wrapped her
arms around herself to try and stop the shivering. It had been
unseasonably mild in London, and she had packed her coat so
that she wouldn't have to carry it. Now she wished she hadn't.
Clearly, the Scottish weather hadn't forgotten that there were
only a couple of weeks to go until Christmas.

Blair was unlocking what looked like a Range Rover,
parked against a wall in the darkness. The back was stacked
with boxes, carrier bags and odd assorted pieces of machinery
and there was only just enough room to wedge Amanda's suitcase behind her seat. 'It looks as if you've been shopping,'
she said brightly as Blair leant across to unlock her door and

she scrambled gratefully into the shelter of the passenger seat. 'Don't tell me they're all Christmas presents!'

'Hardly.' It was obvious that Blair didn't think much of her effort at making conversation and had already written her down as completely inane. He slotted the key into the ignition and coaxed the engine into spluttering life. 'I've merely been taking the opportunity to stock up since I was coming down to town. Dundinnie isn't exactly handy for the shops.'

'So I hear,' said Amanda a little glumly. She loved shops, but Norris had raved about the castle's isolated position. 'The agency warned me,' she explained quickly, feeling Blair glance at her, and then, to divert him, said, 'Is the car all right? It's making an awfully funny noise.' Sue had told her that Blair McAllister was acclaimed as much for his travel documentaries as for his travel books and daring expeditions, and Amanda would have thought that if he was as successful as he was reputed to be then he could afford a car that sounded healthier than this one. Perhaps Norris was closer to the mark in suspecting that Blair had problems trying to maintain a medieval Scottish castle at the same time as financing his travels.

'She's just warming up,' said Blair irritably, as if divining the train of her thoughts. He clicked on the headlights and a powerful beam of light bounced off the wall in front of them and was reflected back through the windscreen, throwing the lean planes of his face into eerie relief. Amanda found herself noticing how the blocks of light and shadow emphasised his profile with its strong nose and clean jawline and lit just one corner of that stern mouth.

Switching on the windscreen wipers, Blair began to reverse the car out of its parking space, but as he rested an arm on her headrest and turned to look through the rear window he caught Amanda watching him and raised one eyebrow in sardonic enquiry. Unaccountably ruffled, Amanda looked quickly away. To her relief, the interior of the car was engulfed in darkness once more as the beam of the headlights swung out and away from the wall. For some stupid reason, she could feel a flush stealing up her cheeks.

'How long will it take us to get to the castle?' she asked with forced brightness, just to show Blair that she hadn't even registered that joltingly brief meeting of their eyes.

'It's normally about two and a half hours,' said Blair, putting the car into first. 'Probably more like three tonight. There was a lot of rain when I drove down this morning, and they were forecasting gales again tonight.'

As if to underline his words, a gust of wind splattered rain against the windscreen. *'Three hours!'* exclaimed Amanda, aghast. 'I could be halfway back to London in that time!'

'Very possibly, but you won't find any nice straight motorways around here. As the crow flies, Dundinnie isn't that far, but we have to follow the road around a couple of lochs and then get through the hills, and there may well be snow up there. It's not an easy road at the best of times, but on a night like this it'll be even slower than usual, so I'm sorry, but you'll just have to be patient.'

He didn't sound very sorry. 'Couldn't we stay here tonight and go tomorrow morning?' pleaded Amanda. She had glanced at a map before she'd set out, measuring the distance against the scale with her thumb, and had calculated that it wouldn't take much more than an hour to get there. That had seemed bad enough after ten hours on the train—and that was before they had been delayed for over an hour. Now the prospect of another three hours seemed too much to bear. 'I've been travelling all day,' she reminded Blair, hoping to appeal to his sense of chivalry, but she might as well have spared her breath.

'You've only been sitting on a train,' he pointed out without a trace of sympathy.

'For eleven and a half hours!' Amanda said indignantly. 'Sitting still for that length of time *is* tiring—or am I only allowed to be tired if I've spent eleven hours hacking through some jungle?'

'If you'd spent eleven *days* hacking through a jungle you'd be entitled to feel tired,' said Blair with a sardonic, sideways glance. 'As far as I can see, all you've been doing is sitting in a first-class carriage not doing anything—not even reading, judging by what you said about my book! I hardly think you've got anything to complain about,' he went on. 'It's not even as if I'm asking you to drive. You can go to sleep if you want.'

'I can't sleep in a car,' said Amanda sulkily. 'It makes me feel sick.'

'In that case you'll just have to stay awake and shut up, won't you?'

He was hateful, she decided, subsiding into simmering silence. Arrogant and inconsiderate and absolutely *hateful*! She had been unfair when she had mentally compared him to Scrooge: Scrooge would have been more charming and certainly better company this Christmas!

She slid a resentful look at Blair from under her lashes. It was all right for him. *He* hadn't been up at the crack of dawn to see Sue and Nigel off at the airport, or had to struggle across London on the tube with a heavy suitcase, and he hadn't had to sit on a train all day with only his crummy book for company either! Anyone with any feelings at all would have taken her to the nearest luxury hotel, poured her a stiff drink and ensured that she had a hot bath before falling into bed. Instead of which she was being dragged on a cross-country marathon and told to shut up when she dared to protest.

Folding her arms, Amanda glowered through the windscreen at the darkness. If Blair wanted her to shut up, she would shut up. She didn't want to waste her conversation on him anyway!

Frustratingly, Blair didn't appear to notice that she was ignoring him. Quite unperturbed by the silence, he drove through the town and out onto the Inverness road. 'The agency tell me that you've had considerable experience of dealing with children,' he said at last as they left the lights of Fort William behind them. 'What made you become a nanny?'

'I started to train as a teacher,' said Amanda, still rather huffily. It was lucky that she knew Sue's career nearly as well as her own. 'But I really liked small children best,' she went on, crossing her fingers in the darkness. 'I used to be a nanny in the holidays and I liked the variety of temporary work. I got to travel more too. Once I spent three weeks in a luxury hotel in the Caribbean.' It was the only one of Sue's jobs that Amanda had ever found the least bit enviable, but Blair McAllister was predictably unimpressed.

'I hope you're not expecting anything like that this time,' he said dampeningly. 'Did the agency explain the situation to you?'

'All they said was that you needed someone to help look after your sister's children,' said Amanda, trying to remember exactly what Sue had told her. 'I gather that she hasn't been well?'

'She's better now, but the illness left her very pulled down, and she really needed a complete break. She went through a very messy divorce last year and I think everything just caught up with her. The children were at school, but there was a very responsible nanny to look after them and she went out to New Zealand to see a friend and have a holiday. Unfortunately, the nanny's mother is very ill, which is why I had to go down and bring the children up here last week. And then we heard that the friend she's staying with has just been involved in an accident, so Belinda feels she ought to stay and help out until she's on her feet again.'

Blair gave a brief sigh. 'Unfortunately, it means that she's not going to be able to get back in time for Christmas and the children are obviously disappointed. I have to admit that I wasn't planning on looking after three children for six weeks, especially when they're having to miss the end of term. That's why I rang your agency. I'm trying to finish a book about my last trip at the moment and, to be frank, I don't know very much about children at the best of times.'

That makes two of us, thought Amanda glumly. 'So you just want someone to keep them out of your way for a bit?'

'I wouldn't put it quite like that,' he said with a stiff look, mistaking her sympathy for accusation. 'But I do have a deadline to meet, and it seemed the best thing for the children to have someone who would know how to look after them properly. They're missing their mother and they haven't had an easy time of it either over the last couple of years and it's made them rather...difficult at times.'

Amanda's heart sank. 'What exactly does ''difficult'' mean?'

'They just don't seem to do any of things we used to do when we were kids. Simon's eleven and Nicholas nearly nine, but all they ever want to do is sit in front of the television.' Blair's voice thinned with disapproval, but Amanda perked up. Watching television didn't sound like being difficult to her.

'There's a little girl too, isn't there?'

'Emily,' he confirmed. 'She's seven and very spoilt. I have to admit that I'll be glad to hand them over to someone who knows how to deal with children,' he added in an unexpected admission. 'If you're half as good as the agency say you are, you should be able to sort them out.'

'Oh, yes.' Amanda's attempt at breezy confidence sounded hollow even to her own ears. 'Yes, of course I will.'

'But you *hate* children!' Sue had exclaimed when Amanda had first proposed her plan.

'Not all of them,' Amanda had defended herself. 'I'm sure I won't mind these children. There are only three of them, after all, and it's not as if they're babies who need their nappies changing all the time.' The two girls had been sitting in a crowded wine bar near Amanda's office. They had managed to find a table and were methodically working their way through the bowl of peanuts that had come with the bottle of wine.

'They still need to be looked after properly,' Sue pointed out.

'I don't see that it can be that difficult,' said Amanda buoyantly. 'You told me yourself that there's a housekeeper to do the cooking, so all I'd have to do is keep an eye on them and stop them falling in the loch.'

'I can't believe you're serious about this!' Sue looked helplessly across the table at her friend. 'You've never had the slightest interest in Scotland and even less in children, and now you say you want to spend several weeks as a nanny in the Highlands! And Christmas too! Surely you'd rather spend it with your family?'

'It's not that I don't want to go home for Christmas,' said Amanda, 'but the job's more important to me at the moment. Anyway,' she added, 'my sister and her three children are going to be there, so the house'll be packed, and everyone will be so busy fussing over them that they won't have time to notice whether I'm there or not.'

'What about Hugh?'

'Oh, that's all off,' said Amanda carelessly. 'He just couldn't understand why I'd rather have a decent job than a mortgage and a screaming baby. He's going out with Lucy now—I'm sure she'll want exactly that and then they'll both be happy,' she added, not without a touch of regret, because Hugh really had been very good-looking. 'No, my future lies in a brilliant career, and if that means spending Christmas in Scotland that's what I'll do.'

'But the whole idea is completely mad!' protested Sue.

Amanda refilled their glasses. 'No, it isn't,' she said confidently. 'It's a brilliant idea. It solves your problem and it solves my problem and it even solves Blair McAllister's problem. What's wrong with that?'

'You don't think it's a bit deceitful?' asked Sue, not without a trace of irony.

'It's not going to make any difference to Blair McAllister which girl he gets,' said Amanda, waving the bottle dismissively. 'He just wants someone to keep an eye on his sister's kids, and I don't see why I shouldn't be able to do that as well as anyone else. I know you think I'm a domestic disaster, but I'm not *completely* irresponsible. And it *would* make a difference to me, Sue,' she went on pleadingly. 'It might be just another job to you, but my entire future depends on getting into Dundinnie Castle!'

Unfortunately, Sue was used to Amanda's sense of drama. 'Your future has depended on so many new jobs that I've lost count!'

'This job's different,' Amanda insisted through a mouthful of peanuts. 'I'm sick of being stuck as a secretary and told that I can only move up the ladder if I stay there for ten years. I want to be successful *now*.'

'There's no point in wanting to be successful unless you know what it is you want to be successful *at*,' said Sue, ever practical, but Amanda brushed that aside.

'Norris knows what I mean. He says he likes people who are hungry for success. That's why he's given me this job. 'If I can get into Dundinnie and convince Blair McAllister to sell, he says there are no limits to how far I can go, but first I've got to prove to him that I've got the killer instinct.'

'The *killer* instinct? You?' Sue regarded her friend with exasperated affection. 'I don't know why you keep up this pretence of wanting to be a ruthless businesswoman when we all know what a softie you are underneath! You'd better not let Norris Jeffries find out about all those lame ducks you sort out if you want him to think that you've got the killer instinct!'

Amanda scowled. She had put a lot of effort into her new

executive image. 'I don't know what you're talking about. I haven't got any lame ducks.'

'No? What about Gerry?'

'She just needs a bit of organisation—' Amanda began defensively, but Sue didn't let her finish.

'And what about that time I turned up on your doorstep in floods of tears when you were on your way to Venice? If you'd had real killer instinct you'd have tossed me a packet of tissues on your way out to the airport, instead of cancelling your whole trip to make sure that Nigel and I got back together.'

'It's because I want you to stay together that I think you should let me take your place,' said Amanda cunningly, seizing her opportunity. 'What's Nigel going to think when you won't give up a crummy temporary job so that you can go with him on this holiday he's won? It's the chance of a lifetime, and he can't turn it down, but if he thinks you don't care enough to want to spent Christmas with him in California, well…' She shook her head sadly. 'It's not as if you'll get many opportunities for a free trip to the States either,' she persevered when Sue looked gloomily down into her glass. 'And just think what he might get up to without you!'

It was obvious that Sue had already thought. 'It's not that I wouldn't love to go…'

'Well, then!' Amanda spread her hands virtuously. 'Here am I, offering to take your place so that you don't let down the agency, and all you can do is think up objections!'

'It's the thought of you taking my place that worries me,' said Sue frankly. 'I've built up a good reputation with the agency, and if they hear that I've let you work for Blair McAllister under false pretences I'm finished. He's a high-profile client. I know you've never read any of his books but you must have seen his programmes.'

'All that pitting-yourself-against-the-elements stuff doesn't really appeal to me,' said Amanda.

'He doesn't just do that,' protested Sue. 'Sometimes it's true, he does take people out into challenging environments—you should have seen what they were doing in Guyana!—but usually it's just his individual view of a country.'

'Maybe, but it never sounds to me as if he goes anywhere with any good restaurants,' said Amanda flippantly. 'What's he supposed to be like?'

'I think he's brilliant. If Nigel hadn't won this holiday, I'd be really looking forward to meeting him.'

Sensing weakness, Amanda sat up straighter. 'The agency won't ever find out,' she said, at her most soothing. 'It's not as if I'm going to *do* anything. All I want is to look round the castle and report back to Norris on its condition. He's set his heart on it for his new health centre, but he only saw it from the outside when he drove past it a couple of months ago. He wants to know what it's like inside so that he can make Blair McAllister a realistic offer.'

'But I thought you said that Norris had already approached him about selling the castle and got a very rude reply telling him to forget the whole idea?'

'Oh, they always say that at first,' said Amanda with all the confidence of one who had been in property development for two whole weeks. 'It's just a way of forcing up the price. That's why Norris needs a report on the inside. He's given me four weeks to get up to the castle and find out what I can about Blair McAllister's financial situation. It's not the sort of place you can turn up to out of the blue, and I was just beginning to think that I'd have to admit that I couldn't do it when you told me you'd been offered a temporary job there starting next week.' Clutching her hands together, she leant pleadingly over the table. 'It can't just be a coincidence, Sue. It has to be *meant*.'

Sue had taken a lot more persuasion, of course, but in the end, as always, Amanda had got her own way. That very morning, she had driven Sue and Nigel to the airport and waved them onto the plane. 'What if something goes wrong?' Sue had wailed, losing her nerve at the last minute.

'Nothing's going to go wrong,' Amanda had said gaily, kissing her goodbye and pushing her firmly towards passport control. 'I'll be able to handle Blair McAllister. It'll be easy—just leave him to me!'

Now she wasn't so sure. She slid a sideways glance at Blair from under her lashes. The dim light from the dashboard instruments was just enough to outline his forceful profile and hint at the inflexible set of his mouth. Watching it, Amanda was conscious of a hollow feeling that there was nothing easy about Blair McAllister and that if there was any handling to be done he would be the one to do it.

Sue's opinion of him had been shared by all the friends whom Amanda had asked, and she had begun to think that she was the only person who hadn't seen his programmes or read his books. He had led some famous expeditions in aid of charity but Amanda's hopes that he would turn out to have a flamboyant personality to match had been firmly quashed. He was tough, intelligent and overwhelmingly competent, they had all agreed. 'But gorgeous!' Pippa, another friend, had added, sighing enviously when she heard where Amanda was going.

Amanda had been inclined to pooh-pooh that idea when she'd first seen a picture of Blair McAllister, but the longer she had studied his photograph, the more she had had to admit that there *was* something intriguing about that air of assurance. Still, he wasn't what *she* would call gorgeous. There was something too unyielding about him, she decided, studying him covertly. He was too cold, too brusque to be really attractive. Then her eyes rested on his mouth and she found herself wondering what it would be like if he turned his head and smiled at her the way he had been smiling in that photograph.

At the thought, an odd, disquieting feeling stirred inside her, and she jerked her gaze away to concentrate on the rhythmic swish and slap of the windscreen wipers. She was supposed to be pretending to be Sue, she reminded herself, and Sue would be moreinterested in the children than in her employer. She cleared her throat. 'Who's looking after the children tonight?'

She thought her voice sounded a little odd, but Blair didn't seem to notice. 'Maggie—my housekeeper—said that she would spend the night since we were going to be so late back. She usually goes home after she's prepared the evening meal. Which reminds me,' he went on tersely, 'you're going to have to help out with the cooking and cleaning. Maggie sprained her wrist very badly yesterday and she won't be able to do much for a while.'

'You want *me* to cook?'

'I cleared it with the agency this morning,' he said, oblivious to Amanda's appalled expression. 'Naturally your salary will reflect the extra work, but the agency said that you wouldn't mind. They told me that you were a good cook.'

Sue was. Sue was calm and patient and didn't work herself into a frenzy when all her pots started to boil at once. Amanda loathed cooking and blessed daily the invention of the microwave. 'I'm not that good,' she said nervously, wondering for one wild moment if she could sprain her wrist too.

'It doesn't need to be anything fancy. Good, plain food is all those children need.'

Amanda's heart sank even further. If there was one thing she hated more than cooking, it was good, plain food. In cuisine, as in life, she liked things as fancy as possible. Lapsing back into glum silence, she contemplated the rain which was now slashing against the car while the wind whooped and swirled judderingly around them. It looked as if it was going to be a very dull Christmas.

CHAPTER TWO

'WHY do you call yourself Amanda instead of Susan?' asked Blair suddenly out of the darkness.

'Amanda's my middle name,' said Amanda, who had anticipated that question.

'What's wrong with Susan? It's not as if it's an embarrassing name.'

Of course, she should have just said that she preferred Amanda and left it at that, but Amanda had always had a taste for the dramatic and had never been able to resist the temptation to embellish a story. Her elaborate excuses for being late had been famous at school. 'All the girls in my family are called Susan,' she improvised. 'We use our middle names so that we don't get confused.'

'You're *all* called Susan?' She could feel the disbelief in the glance he shot her. 'What on earth for?'

'After my great-great-grandmother,' said Amanda fluently, grateful as always for her ability to tell the most enormous fibs with a straight face. 'She was a missionary.' In the darkness it was impossible to read Blair's expression, but she could sense his scepticism and it put her on her mettle. 'In the South Pacific,' she added as a bit of corroborative detail.

It was a mistake. 'Oh?' said Blair. 'Where in the South Pacific?'

She had forgotten that he probably knew the South Pacific as well as she knew the Number 9 bus route. Feverishly, Amanda tried to think of the name of an island but, as so often when forced to call upon memory rather than imagination, her mind remained blank. 'She moved around a lot,' she said vaguely instead, but as this sounded rather dull she was unable

22

to resist adding a touch of drama to the story. 'Family legend has it that she was eaten by cannibals,' she added, lowering her voice to just the right touch of reverence. 'One day she got into her canoe and paddled off to a new island, and she was never seen again.'

'Really?' Blair's voice dripped disbelief and Amanda sighed inwardly. Perhaps it hadn't been a very convincing story.

Oh, well, she had enjoyed it, anyway. As she had talked, the mythical Susan had become almost real to her, but it was clear that Blair lacked the fertile imagination that had been getting her into trouble since she'd been a child. Life would be much simpler if she'd only learn to keep it under control, she acknowledged, but not nearly so much fun.

Outside, the storm was growing wilder, driving rain ferociously into the windscreen. Blair's body was utterly relaxed, but his grip on the steering wheel was sure as he held the car steady against the gusting wind. Amanda wished that she could relax enough to fall asleep, but there was something unsettling about Blair's massive, silent presence, like a barrier between her and the storm.

He had ignored her after the story about her supposed ancestor and Amanda, normally the most confidently chatty of people, had found herself unable to think of anything to say to break the silence. She was too aware of the cramped confines of the car. Outside it was very dark. The dashboard lights were reflected in her window, but otherwise there was nothing. Blair seemed very close, almost overwhelming, and she wished that she didn't notice every time he moved his hand to the gear lever or glanced across to see if she was still awake.

Once they had turned off the Inverness road, they hardly saw another car, and to Amanda it seemed as if they were driving interminably into the darkness while the rain turned to sleet, zooming in at the windscreen like a meteor shower. In spite of herself, her head began to loll forward. She had no idea how much time had passed when the sound of the car splashing through a huge puddle along with the sound of Blair swearing under his breath jerked her into consciousness. 'What's the matter?' she asked blearily, struggling upright in her seat as the car began to splutter alarmingly.

'Water in the petrol,' he said curtly. He changed down, but his attempts to rev the engine had little effect and not much further down the road the car coughed sadly to a halt.

Blair swore again and hauled on the handbrake. 'That's all I need,' he muttered, and reached across Amanda without ceremony to rummage in the glove box.

Very conscious of his nearness, she shrank back in her seat so that she didn't have to touch him more than necessary...not that he even seemed to notice that she was there! It was a relief when his fingers closed around a torch and he sat back, but the next minute he was opening his door.

'Where are you going?'

'Out for a stroll.'

Amanda stared stupidly at him as the rain slashed against the windows, wondering if she had fallen asleep after all and this was just a bizarre dream. 'A stroll? In *this*?'

Blair gave a short, exasperated sigh. 'Of course not!' he said irritably. 'I'm going to clean the filter, what do you think? And, what's more, you're coming with me.'

'Me?' She came to abruptly. 'But I don't know anything about cars!'

'You don't need to be a mechanic to hold a torch.'

'But...' Amanda glanced helplessly from the rain to her city suit. 'I'll get soaked!' she wailed, but if she had hoped to rouse Blair's chivalrous instincts she was doomed to disappointment.

'I dare say, but the sooner we get out there, the sooner we can both get dry,' he said. He had half closed his door, but now he made as if to open it again. 'Now, are you coming?'

Amanda was looking nervously out at the wild night. 'Are you sure this is wise?'

'What do you mean?' asked Blair, exasperated.

'I've seen horror films like this,' she said. 'You know the kind of thing…a couple break down in an isolated place on a night just like this, and as soon as they get out of the car you want to shout at them not to be so stupid, because you know that some monster is lurking in the darkness, and it's going to creep up on them and grab the girl—no, the man,' she corrected herself after a moment's thought. 'That way the girl has to cope by herself. Then you just hear the man screaming and lots of horrible crunching sounds, and then *she* starts screaming, and instead of being sensible and getting back inside the car and locking the doors she runs off into the darkness, and the monster stalks her and—'

'Amanda?'

Carried away by her own story, Amanda had been unaware of Blair's incredulous expression. Now she stopped in surprise as his deceptively gentle voice cut across her ramble. 'Yes?' she said, a little disorientated by the abrupt switch from imagination to reality.

He handed her the torch. 'Shut up,' he said, quietly but very distinctly, and got out of the car.

'Don't blame me when the monster gets you,' grumbled Amanda, but she opened her door. A gust of wind and rain swirled into the car, and she shivered. It looked awfully dark out there. She could just make out Blair's figure silhouetted against the headlights.

'Come on!' he shouted, beckoning irritably.

Completely unnerved by her own story, Amanda hesitated, but Blair seemed more of an immediate threat than the monster so she climbed awkwardly out of the car and tittuped round the front of the car in her unsuitable shoes, her face screwed up against the weather. Blinking the rain out of her eyes, she huddled under the meagre protection of the bonnet, where Blair was already leaning over the engine.

'Over here,' he ordered. He had to shout over the scream of the wind. 'I can't see a thing without the torch.'

Reluctantly, Amanda edged towards him. In the wavering light, she could see Blair regarding her with intense exasperation. 'How am I supposed to see anything with you waving the torch around from over there?' he demanded when she stopped uncertainly, and reached out a hard hand to grab her by the waist and drag her into his side.

Amanda half fell against him with a squeak of surprise. 'Now, hold it there,' said Blair, putting his hand around hers and pointing the torch at the filter. 'This is a fiddly job and I need to be able to see what I'm doing.'

He turned back to the engine without another word. Amanda tried to hold the torch steady, but her hand was already numb with cold. She felt oddly breathless. Even through the buffeting wind and rain, she was very conscious of the granite solidity of Blair's body where she was pressed against him.

'We must stop meeting like this!' she bent to shout in his ear, trying to make a joke of it.

'What?'

Blair lifted his head to stare at her, and Amanda was disconcerted to find that his face was very close. The rain had already sleeked his hair against his head and a trickle of water was making its way from his temple down one lean cheek.

'Joke,' she explained. 'Just trying to lighten the atmosphere.'

He sighed against her. 'I'm glad you're having such a good time, of course, but do you think you could keep the jokes until we're back inside the car?'

'Just trying to help,' she muttered, sulking at his sarcastic response. Just as she had thought: no sense of humour.

'If you want to help, Amanda, I suggest you keep that torch still and stop distracting me!' said Blair unpleasantly.

She was left staring resentfully down at the back of his head. It was very cold and the sleet was rapidly turning to snow. Her teeth were soon clattering together uncontrollably. To distract herself, she began mentally rewriting the blurb about Blair that had appeared on the dust-jacket of his book. 'Brilliant', 'extraordinary' and 'stimulating' could go for a start, to be replaced by 'grumpy', 'boring' and 'downright disagreeable'.

Her eyes rested crossly on what she could see of his face as she thought of a few more adjectives to describe the *real* Blair McAllister. Unaware of her regard, he was frowning down at the engine, his expression absorbed. The dim glow of reflected torchlight caught the sheen of wet skin and glimmered over the hard line of his cheek.

Suddenly, Amanda found that instead of thinking about how much she disliked him she was thinking about the feel of his body, about the strength of his arm pulling her against him, about the warmth of his fingers around hers as he steadied the torch. She tried to distract herself by thinking about the wonderful career that Norris had promised her, but the slick city office with its frantically bleeping phones and constant buzz of pressure seemed unutterably remote from this moment, as she huddled against a man she had met only a couple of hours ago while the wind plastered her wet skirt against her legs and the rain ran coldly down her neck and the only warmth and security in the world lay in the hard strength of Blair McAllister's body.

With an effort, she looked away from him, but the wind blew the rain in her eyes if she faced in any other direction, and although she tried staring down at the engine instead her eyes kept skittering back to his face. He had turned his head slightly as he squinted at the filter and she could see the corner of his mouth. It gave her a strange feeling. She had forgotten that she was rehearsing all the things she disliked about him. All she could do was watch his mouth and wonder if it would feel as cool and firm as it looked.

Aghast at the direction of her thoughts, Amanda stiffened. What on earth had made her think about *that*? All at once, her senses were jangling with a humiliating awareness of the

oblivious man beside her. *He* wasn't bothered by the feel of
her body pressed close against him, or distracted by the curve
of her mouth. As far as Blair was concerned, she was just an
irritating extension of his torch. She shifted her feet so that
she could hold herself rigidly away from him but she doubted
whether he even noticed, and it didn't stop her tensing with
every move he made.

Shaking with cold, Amanda stood awkwardly arched over
the engine like a lamppost. She was so ridiculously, inexpli-
cably nervous that when Blair suddenly reached across her to
the other side of the engine she jerked back in an instinctive
attempt not to come into contact with the body that had left
her feeling so on edge. The sudden movement knocked the
torch against the edge of the bonnet and out of her nerveless
fingers, and before she had a chance to retrieve it it crashed
down onto the tarmac where it promptly went out.

'What the—!' Blair straightened furiously to glare at her.
'Where's the torch?'

Amanda groped around on the road until she found it, but
when she tried to click it on again nothing happened.

'That's a great help!' He snatched it from her, cursing under
his breath as he shook it savagely. 'Damn! The bulb's gone.
I'll have to go and get another one. You stay here,' he added
as an afterthought. 'And try not to do any more damage if you
can help it!'

Mortified, Amanda hunched wretchedly under the bonnet as
Blair made his way round to the driver's seat. She could see
the sleet driving across the straight beam of the headlights but
beyond that there was only the howling wind and pitch-
darkness, and she thought of the monster that she had described so glibly in the safety of the car. She hadn't thought
of it at all when she had had Blair beside her, but now she
felt cold and scared and very vulnerable.

The seconds stretched interminably. What was Blair *doing*?
He could at least say something to let her know that he was

still there. Anything might have happened to him; anything might have snuck up in the darkness. Amanda's imagination, always vivid, spun out of control, and she had worked herself into such a state that when the lights snapped abruptly off, plunging her into blackness, she gasped and began to grope her way frantically round the bonnet in the direction where Blair had disappeared.

Gibbering with fear, she had just made it to the corner when she came slap up against a hard body. In spite of herself, she shrieked.

'What the hell do you think you're doing?' Blair's voice demanded furiously.

Amanda clutched at him in relief. 'Oh, thank God it's you! What happened?'

'What do you mean, *what happened*? Nothing happened!'

'But the lights went out!'

'I switched them off to save the battery.' Blair had obviously never watched any films where the hero put his arms comfortingly around the heroine. He put Amanda away from him in an irritable gesture. 'I couldn't find another bulb, so we'll have to wait until it's light now.'

Amanda stood feeling rather foolish and wishing she could forget how reassuring it had been to hold onto him. 'I thought something had happened to you,' she tried to explain.

'What could possibly happen to me between the engine and the steering wheel? And don't start on that silly monster business!' he added in an acerbic voice before she had a chance to answer.

'Stranger things have happened,' she muttered darkly as Blair moved past her in the dark to slam down the bonnet.

'The worst that's going to happen to you is that you're going to get even wetter if you stand out here any longer,' he pointed out in a crushing voice. 'So I suggest you stop wittering and get in the car.'

'Can you turn on the lights again?' she pleaded. It was so

dark that she couldn't even see Blair and she edged closer
along the car towards the sound of his voice. 'I can't see a
thing.'

'Feel your way round the bonnet,' Blair began, but, as if
against his better judgement, he reached out into the blackness
until his hand brushed against hers. Amanda clutched at it
thankfully. 'Here,' he said gruffly, leading her round to the
other side of the car and opening the passenger door. 'You'd
better get in.'

The opening of the door gave her enough light to climb in
out of the storm, but Amanda was strangely reluctant to let go
of his hand. 'Thank you,' she said humbly.

Moving confidently through the pitch-dark, Blair was bang-
ing his own door shut only moments later. He reached up to
click on the overhead light and began stripping off his jacket.
'Well, we seem to have survived the monsters against all the
odds. Or are they circling the car even now, slavering in anticipation at the thought of us both trapped here?'

'Very funny,' said Amanda, unappreciative of his sarcasm,
but she locked her door anyway. She watched him toss his
sodden jacket over the boxes in the back and run a hand over
his wet hair before wiping the worst of the rain from his face.
In the dim light she could see a trickle still heading down
towards his jaw and for one extraordinary moment even considered reaching across to stop it with her finger. Her hand
tingled with the thought and she looked abruptly away. 'What
do we do now?' she asked, clearing her throat.

'Wait.'

No one could accuse Blair McAllister of garrulity, Amanda
thought with an inward sigh. 'Is that it?' she said after a moment.

'Unless you can do mechanics by Braille, yes,' he said
tersely. 'If you hadn't dropped that torch, we could be on our
way by now. What made you drop it, anyway?' he went on,
turning in his seat to look at her. 'One minute you were stand-

ing there quietly, and the next you were jumping around like a scalded cat.'

'I was cold,' said Amanda, who had no intention of telling him why she had been so tense. 'My hands were numb. It was like the North Pole out there.' She shivered and wrapped her arms around her body. 'It's like the North Pole in here, come to that.'

'It's nothing like the North Pole,' said Blair impatiently. Of course, he *would* have been there, wouldn't he? He leant closer and touched the sodden material of her suit. 'You're soaking!' His voice was suddenly sharp. 'You'd better get that suit off.'

'I bet you say that to all the girls,' she muttered.

'Only when I've known them longer than two hours,' he said. His face was quite straight, but amusement threaded his voice and when Amanda looked at him suspiciously one corner of his mouth twitched.

For some reason, she felt a blush stealing up her cheeks. She felt ridiculously ruffled. This was Blair McAllister, she reminded herself with an edge of desperation. All he had done was smile at her—and not even a proper smile at that!—so why was she having trouble breathing properly?

'I'll get your suitcase out,' he was saying with a return to his usual manner. Leaning over the seat, he manoeuvred her case so that it was lying flat on top of the boxes behind her. 'I suggest you take off those wet things first, and then find something warm and dry to put on instead.'

'Yes…yes, I'll do that.' Amanda pulled herself together with an effort. She must be even more tired than she had thought to let a smile—a suggestion of a smile—discompose her. She leant forward to struggle out of her jacket, but she was so cold that Blair had to help her, and the feel of his hands grazing against her only made her more awkward.

'That shirt's sodden too,' he said when he eventually managed to peel off the jacket and spread it out in the back. 'Go on, take that off too. There's no point in being modest if it means you dying of pneumonia, and if you're worried about me, I have had a very long, trying day, not improved by hanging around at the station for an hour and half or breaking down, and I can assure you that seduction is the last thing on my mind!'

'The thought never occurred to me,' said Amanda stiffly through chattering teeth.

Blair sat back in his seat and studied the bedraggled figure beside him. The meagre light was enough to see that the shiny brown hair was plastered to her head and as he watched she sniffed and drearily wiped a trickle of rain from her nose in an unconscious gesture of tiredness. 'Come on, hurry up before you freeze to death,' he said almost brusquely. 'It's not exactly the ideal situation for a spot of lovemaking anyway, is it?' he went on casually as Amanda began to fumble with the tiny buttons of her shirt. 'I prefer a little more comfort myself.'

Amanda tried to imagine the dour Blair McAllister making love and found to her discomfort that she could manage it with unnerving clarity. She had known the man for something less than three hours, had seen him clearly for less than three minutes...how was it that she could picture him so vividly, reaching out, leaning over, bending down for a kiss? What made her picture him with a slow smile and slow, sure hands?

Her fingers were still numb with cold, and the distracting image of Blair was making her even clumsier as she struggled awkwardly with the buttons. They were tricky at the best of times and she muttered with a mixture of embarrassment and frustration as her hands slipped again.

'Here, let me have a go,' said Blair abruptly, and before Amanda quite realised what was happening he had leant over to undo the top button. He must have been as cold as she was, but his fingers were deft and impersonal, and warm where they brushed against her skin.

Amanda was intensely grateful for the dim light that disguised the wave of colour that swept up her cheeks. Her fingers might be numb with cold, but inside she could feel herself burning with an excruciating awareness of the man so impersonally unbuttoning her shirt with fingers that were just as slow and sure as she had imagined.

'Seduction is the last thing on my mind,' he had said, but she couldn't stop herself wondering what it would be like if it wasn't. What would it be like if he was thinking about making love now, what if he was thinking about her? What if he were unbuttoning her shirt like a lover and not like a nanny undressing a tiresome child? What would it be like if he slid his hands beneath the silk to caress her skin? Amanda's heart was thudding slowly, painfully against her ribs and her throat was tight and dry. God, what was the matter with her? She must stop this; she must—

'I must choose a more comfortable place to undress you next time,' said Blair. 'This would be much more fun if we were both warm and dry and weren't squashed into the front seat of a damp car, wouldn't it?' The sound of his voice wrenched her back to reality, but she heard only the undercurrent of laughter in his voice and stared blankly at him.

'Joke,' he quoted her own explanation back at her. 'Just trying to lighten the atmosphere.'

Amanda swallowed and smiled weakly. If only he knew how close he had been to reading her mind! 'It's just as well the seats are so wet, then, isn't it?' she said feebly as Blair undid the last button and pulled the shirt off her to reveal the dull gleam of the cream silk camisole she wore.

'Just as well,' he said after a moment.

There was a long pause, and then he looked up directly into Amanda's eyes. The light wasn't good enough to read his expression. It threw a fuzzy glow over one side of his face, blurring the forceful features but paradoxically heightening the impression of granite strength that already seemed so much a part of him. In the darkness he was a massive presence, at once reassuring and disturbing.

Amanda was held, pinned by that unreadable gaze. The rain drumming on the roof and the whooping wind seemed to be coming from a long way away. There was only the darkness and the blurry light on Blair's cheek and Blair's jaw and the solid line of Blair's throat.

She never knew how long they looked at each other. It might only have been a few seconds, but suddenly he was looking away and she realised that she had been holding her breath. She let it out with a tiny gasp and, as if released from a spell, scrambled round in her seat to scrabble through her suitcase. She couldn't distinguish any colours but that didn't matter. All that mattered was to put on as many layers as possible to act as barriers between her and Blair McAllister's unsettling gaze.

Her fingers closed on the cashmere jumper that her mother had given her last Christmas and she tugged it out, grateful for its soft warmth. After several false starts, she discovered a shirt and dragged it on before wriggling out of her wet skirt and tights and wriggling into some leggings and two pairs of socks to warm her frozen feet. Heaven only knew what colours she had on or whether any of it matched, but Amanda, studiously avoiding Blair's eyes, cared only that she was covered.

'Have you got a towel in there?' Blair asked when she had finished.

'I think so…somewhere.' Kneeling on the seat, she groped through her suitcase until she found it. 'Here.'

Blair took it and, ordering Amanda to bend her head, towelled her hair vigorously until she protested. She emerged complaining bitterly and with her hair standing up in all directions, but had to admit that she felt better. Grumbling about Blair's rough treatment had dispersed her awkwardness too, and it was possible now to see that her earlier bizarre reaction to him had merely been the result of cold and exhaustion.

'Better?' he asked as he rubbed the towel over his own hair.

'Well, *drier*,' she admitted cautiously. 'All I need now is a hot meal, a stiff drink and a warm bed and I'd be really quite comfortable.'

'I can't do much about the hot meal or the warm bed,' said Blair, reaching in the back for a carrier bag, which he extracted at last with a grunt of satisfaction. 'But I can provide a drink.' He produced a bottle from the bag as he eased himself back into his seat. 'Do you like whisky?'

'Haven't you got anything else?' said Amanda, who had been hoping that he might magically produce a bottle of red and a corkscrew. She might have known that he would be a whisky man.

'No,' he said, and unscrewed the top. 'Have some of this anyway. It'll warm you up.'

'Oh, all right.' He passed her the bottle and Amanda reached for it without enthusiasm. Her fingers fumbled against his and she couldn't prevent a tiny frisson shivering down her spine. 'Sorry,' she said awkwardly.

'Have you got a good grip of it before I let go?' asked Blair. 'I don't want a good bottle of malt going the same way as the torch!'

The astringency in his voice helped Amanda to ignore the strumming sensation where their hands had touched. 'I wouldn't dream of dropping anything quite so close to your heart,' she said with a frosty look. Taking a defiantly large swig, she promptly choked and spluttered as the whisky burned down her throat.

'That's better, isn't it?' said Blair as she shook her head to clear it and hastily handed back the bottle.

'It's certainly...warming,' gasped Amanda hoarsely.

'Warming? Is that all you can say? That's Macallan single malt you were chucking back!'

'Is that good?'

'The best.'

'Oh, dear, I hope you weren't saving it for a special occasion.'

Blair drank reflectively from the bottle. 'A whisky like this makes any occasion special,' he said.

'What, even stranded in the middle of a storm with a hysterical nanny?' Amanda asked ironically, and he turned in his seat to look at her. Her hair stuck out in every direction where he had rubbed it dry, but her eyelashes were still spiky with rain. Without the suit and the sleek hairstyle she looked a lot less than her twenty-four years, and almost unrecognisable as the smart young woman who had got off the train at Fort William. Blair's eyes rested on her face, still somehow vivid in the dim light, and the chin which was tilted at a characteristically challenging angle.

'Even that,' he said slowly, faint amusement bracketing his mouth.

What *was* it about that damned elusive smile of his that made the blood tingle beneath her skin? Amanda turned away to rest her cheek against the window and let the cool glass drain the heat from her face. 'I'm glad you're finding it special,' she muttered. 'I can think of other ways to describe being stuck out in the middle of nowhere, trapped in a wet car by slavering monsters and only a bottle of whisky for comfort!'

'Come on, stop complaining,' said Blair without heat. 'Things could be worse.'

'How?'

'You could be outside with your monsters, for a start. You ought to be grateful that we've the car for shelter. At least you'll be able to sleep.'

'Sleep? *Sleep?*' Amanda's voice rose to an outraged squeak as exhaustion caught up with her. 'How can I possibly sleep when I'm tired and I'm cold and I'm hungry and I wish I'd never come near bloody Scotland in the first place?'

Blair was unmoved by her outburst. 'Have another drink,' was all he said, and he handed her the bottle. Amanda was ready for the fiery impact of the whisky this time and took a more cautious slug. 'I've even got some biscuits,' he added, producing a packet out of the bag by his feet. 'So that will cross hunger off your list of miseries.' He ripped open the packet and passed it over to Amanda.

'A ginger-nut wasn't quite what I had in mind,' she sighed, taking three anyway. She bit into one glumly. 'I was thinking of something warm and tasty, preferably smothered in cheese, accompanied by a bottle of wine and followed by a nice, fattening pudding. Sticky toffee pudding,' she decided after a moment's thought. Munching on the biscuit, she lapsed into silence and stared disconsolately out at the rain which was still being hurled out of the darkness by a frustrated gale.

Blair regarded her with a sort of exasperated amusement for a moment and then reached up to click off the overhead light. 'We may as well save the battery until we need it,' he said as the darkness blotted out everything. Amanda couldn't even see her ginger-nut.

'You're not a very typical nanny, are you?' His voice came out of the blackness, deep and strong and infinitely reassuring.

'What do you mean?' said Amanda cautiously.

'I always imagine nannies to be calm, practical people, used to coping when things go wrong.'

'I'm coping!' she ruffled up instantly.

'Not without making a fuss,' Blair pointed out astringently. 'What would you be like if this was a crisis?'

'What do you mean, *if*? This is a crisis!'

'You've just proved my point for me,' he said, sounding resigned. 'You've got to spend a few uncomfortable hours in the car. It's perfectly safe, you've got dry clothes, something to drink, something to eat and me to look after you in the unlikely event that anything *did* happen, but, for you, that's a crisis! What would you do if something really bad happened to you?'

'Right at this moment, I can't think of anything worse than

being stuck here with you,' said Amanda sourly, and deliberately drank some more of his precious whisky.

Blair ignored that. 'I just hope that you're a little less...*extravagant* when it comes to dealing with children,' he said disapprovingly. 'Judging by what the agency told me, I can only assume that you undergo some sort of personality change when actually faced with a child!'

In the darkness, Amanda put up her chin defiantly. 'Well, we'll see, won't we?'

'Yes,' said Blair. He was no more than a black blur against more blackness but Amanda could feel that uncomfortably acute gaze resting on her. She just hoped he couldn't see in the dark, or her expression would surely give her away! 'We'll see.'

CHAPTER THREE

AMANDA'S head was aching. Opening one eye very cautiously, she found herself looking at something dark and curved only inches away from her face. She stared at it for a long time before her pounding brain registered that she was looking at the bottom of a steering wheel.

It hurt too much to think about what it was doing there. Amanda closed her eye again, but the effort of recognising a steering wheel had set her mind working, albeit slowly, and as she lay and willed herself to sink back into comfortable oblivion memories of the night before came filtering back in a series of odd, unconnected pictures: huddling under the bonnet in the sluicing rain, spluttering as the whisky burned down her throat, sitting very still as Blair undid the buttons of her shirt and being passionately glad of the darkness.

Blair... Until then, Amanda had been remembering in the peculiarly detached way of the half-asleep, but his image dissolved the last wisps of dream and brought her awake with a jolt. At the same moment, she became aware that fingers were twisting strands of her hair absently together and her eyes snapped open with the sudden realisation that she was sprawled across the front of the car with her head in Blair McAllister's lap. His other hand was resting lightly at the curve of her hip, and his thighs were broad and firm and relaxed beneath her cheek.

'At last!' Blair must have felt her involuntary stiffening. 'I thought you were going to sleep all morning.'

'I didn't realise...' Horribly embarrassed, Amanda struggled upright, wincing at the stiffness of her limbs. Someone—presumably Blair—had stuffed a couple of jumpers from her suit-

case around the handbrake, but it hadn't stopped it digging
into her. 'Y-you should have woken me,' she stammered.

'I didn't have the heart,' said Blair. 'You were sleeping like
a baby.'

She blinked at him, disconcerted to find him at once a
stranger and oddly familiar. For the first time she registered
that it was light. The darkness of the night before had blurred
the strength of his features and now, in the brightness of morning, it was as if she had never seen his face before.

It was his eyes she noticed first of all. They were an opaque
blue-grey, the colour of slate, and beneath dark, sarcastic-
looking eyebrows they held an unnervingly acute expression
that gave focus to his face. For Amanda, it was as if the morning light had thrown everything about him into sharp relief:
the angle of his jaw, the thick, dark hair, the prickle of stubble
on his unshaven skin and, most of all, the way his mouth was
set in a line that was already uncannily unfamiliar.

Aware that she was staring, and afflicted by sudden shyness,
Amanda looked away. 'I don't feel as if I slept a wink,' she
said uncomfortably.

'You slept more than a wink,' said Blair. 'You drank half
my whisky, keeled over into my lap in the middle of a sen-
tence and proceeded to snore for the rest of the night.'

Amanda looked appalled. 'I didn't, did I?' She did vaguely
remember drinking whisky out of a bottle, but she had no
recollection of falling asleep at all. She looked suspiciously at
Blair. 'Anyway, I don't snore.'

'It sounded remarkably like snoring to me.' His voice was
sardonic, not unamused. 'I've been listening to you ever since
the wind dropped, so I should know. Still, I suppose I should
be glad that one of us at least had a comfortable night.'

'If someone asked me to describe my first night in Scotland,
comfortable wouldn't be the first word that sprang to mind,'
said Amanda sourly, grimacing as she stretched her stiff limbs.
'I feel terrible.'

'I'm not surprised, judging by the amount of my whisky you sank last night. I thought you weren't supposed to like the stuff?'

Amanda held her aching head. 'I don't.' With her other hand, she twisted round the rear-view mirror and peered blearily into it. Her hair had lost its customary bounce and shine in last night's rain and, although now dry, it stood up at impossible angles around her face, one side of which was marked with narrow red lines where her cheek had been pressed into Blair's cords. Mascara was smudged beneath her gritty eyes and she moaned as she rubbed it away with a knuckle. 'Ugh!' was all she felt capable of groaning, and, unable to bear the sight of herself any longer, she turned the mirror away.

'I must say that you don't look quite as smart as you did when you got off the train last night.' Blair pretended to look Amanda over critically, but she could tell that he was enjoying himself. He didn't actually smile, but amusement lurked around his mouth and the crinkles at the corners of his eyes deepened. Involuntarily, she followed his gaze from the scarlet cashmere jumper, which she had managed to put on back to front, to the hideously clashing leggings and on down to the assortment of odd socks which she had pulled on last night in her haste to cover herself.

Some executive she looked now! Mortified, Amanda hurriedly pulled off her jumper and put it back on the right way round, making sure this time that both sides of her shirt collar lay neatly over the round neck. The small detail made her feel better and she patted the collar down, only to flush as she caught Blair's mocking slate eyes.

'What time is it?' she asked crossly.

He glanced at his watch and told her.

Amanda shuddered. 'I knew I wouldn't like it,' she grumbled, rubbing a hand round her aching neck.

'Your previous charges must have been very well behaved if you're not used to getting up at this sort of time,' said Blair,

callously indifferent to her suffering. He reached down to release the bonnet and opened his door. 'Not that I'd call this
particularly early. It would count as a lie-in on an expedition.'

'Remind me never to join one of your expeditions,' muttered Amanda, watching him morosely as he jumped out and
went round to inspect the engine. Still grumbling to herself,
she opened her own door and eased herself out to stand in the
road in her mismatched socks and stretch painfully. Only then
did she look round her and her jaw dropped.

They had spluttered to a halt on a long, straight stretch of
road that swept down the hillside to the shores of a loch which
was as smooth and still as dark glass below them. The fury
of last night's storm might never have been. Not a breath of
wind stirred the surface of the water, and it reflected back the
massive snow-capped peaks looming around it, sharply out-
lined against a clear, crisp sky. Amanda, whose image of
Scotland until now had been of brown hills shrouded in grey
mist, could only stare at the scene spread out before her like
a vast postcard. The hills were a warm golden colour, separ-
ated from the blue of the sky by their crowns of white snow,
and the crystalline light made her blink.

'Oh,' she said.

Blair glanced up from the engine. 'It's quite a view to wake
up to, isn't it?'

'Ye-es.' She looked slowly around her once more, her
breath freezing in a white cloud. She didn't think that she had
ever seen anywhere as empty as this before. The thin ribbon
of road stretching out into the distance was the only sign of
civilisation; other than that, there were only hills and sky and
water and cold, clear air. There was something overwhelming
about the austere grandeur of the scene that made Amanda
feel very small. The massive, uncompromising mountains reminded her of Blair, she decided, trying to shrug off the feeling. 'It's all a bit bleak, isn't it?'

He looked disapproving at her lack of enthusiasm. 'It's magnificent country. You're very lucky to see it like this.'

But Amanda was in no mood to admire the scenery. After the first shock of surprise, she had lapsed back into early-morning disgruntlement. 'I feel a lot of things right now,' she sighed, 'but lucky is not one of them.'

She was dying to go to the loo, but trees or bushes seemed to be in short supply up here. For miles there seemed to be nothing but tussocky grass interspersed with clumps of heather, dead, battered bracken and the odd patch of unmelted snow. Peeling off her ridiculous socks, Amanda rummaged in her case for a pair of trainers. She was tempted to change all her clothes, but it didn't seem worth it before she had a bath, and anyway, she was damned if she was going to undress in front of Blair McAllister in broad daylight. It had been awkward enough in the dark!

There was a granite outcrop in the heather further up the hill. Deciding that it offered the best privacy she was going to get, Amanda began to clamber up the steep bank that ran along the roadside.

'Where do you think you're going?' asked Blair, straightening from the engine.

She pointed at the outcrop. 'Just up there.'

'What on earth for?'

'Why do you think?' she said testily.

He sighed. 'Why don't you just go behind the car? I won't look.'

'Someone else might,' she pointed out, grabbing onto a clump of heather so that she could haul herself up onto the top of the bank at last.

'Who?' he demanded impatiently. 'In case you hadn't noticed, there's not exactly a constant stream of traffic along this road.'

'A car might come round the corner any minute.'

'Amanda, the nearest corner is a good five miles away!

You'd have plenty of time to gather yourself together if you're that inhibited.'

'I am not inhibited!' she snapped, irritated by his attitude. 'I simply prefer a little privacy, and if I want to hide behind a rock I will.' Turning her back on him, she attempted to stalk off, but it was hard to stalk with dignity through knee-high tussocks of grass and heather, and she ended up ploughing inelegantly through it. It wasn't long before she was regretting her determined stand. The outcrop which had looked so close from the road seemed to keep receding up the hill, and by the time she had struggled up to it she was exhausted.

To make matters worse, the granite turned out to be a sheer face set into the hillside, offering virtually no protection anyway, and she was still clearly visible from the road. Gasping for breath, Amanda could see Blair calmly tinkering with the engine, but even as she glowered resentfully down at him he glanced up the hill and saw her.

'Are you planning to spend all day up there?' he shouted, and tapped his watch significantly with his spanner.

Amanda didn't deign to answer and wouldn't have had the breath for it anyway. Instead she turned her back with something suspiciously like a flounce and tried to make herself as insignificant as possible against the granite—a hard job when you were wearing a scarlet jumper. She might as well have had a flashing neon sign over her head.

Getting down the hill was nearly as bad as getting up it. The heather caught at her leggings and the laces of her trainers, and when the slope flattened near the bank she trod in a bog, thereby ruining yet another pair of shoes and her temper.

'Feeling better?' Blair asked sarcastically as she scrambled clumsily down onto the road once more. He had been watching her progress as he leant against the car with folded arms.

'No, I am not!' stormed Amanda, wiping her soggy trainers savagely on some dead bracken and convinced in some obscure way that it was all Blair McAllister's fault. 'To be quite frank with you, I wish I'd never come to Scotland. The last few hours have been the worst of my life. I'll be lucky if I don't get pneumonia after last night, I'm so stiff I'll probably never walk properly again, all I've had to eat is a few ginger-nuts and now I'll have to go barefoot for the rest of the month,' she finished childishly.

Blair tutted. 'I'm not surprised Hugh dumped you if you were always this bad-tempered in the morning,' he said.

'Anyone would be bad-tempered if they'd spent the night I had! And, anyway, Hugh—' Amanda stopped abruptly. 'How do you know about Hugh?' she demanded.

'You told me about him at length last night, just before you passed out,' said Blair with a sardonic look. 'I heard all about how attractive he was and how he had taken up with some "drip"—your description, not mine—but really, you thought it was probably for the best because he never understood about your career and thought you should have wanted to settle down and have babies.' Blair's voice mimicked her so clearly that she squirmed inwardly.

'I can't think why I told you all that,' she mumbled.

'I assumed that you weren't used to neat whisky,' said Blair. 'I certainly hope you don't make a habit of confiding your life history to virtual strangers!'

Amanda stared at him, aghast at her own indiscretion. 'Oh, dear, I must have been terribly boring,' she said nervously. What if she had told him the truth about taking Sue's place? He would have said something, though, wouldn't he? she re-assured herself. Blair McAllister wasn't the kind of man who would calmly accept an impostor.

His next words seemed to confirm that however indiscreet she had been she hadn't been *that* indiscreet. 'No, I found it fascinating,' he said, although not without some sarcasm. 'I didn't realise that anyone would think of nannying as a career incompatible with children. I would have thought that anyone who chose to spend their time looking after other people's children would want to have their own eventually. Isn't that what you want?'

Amanda thought of a recent weekend that she had spent with her sister, who had three children under five, and barely repressed a shudder. 'No...I mean, not yet,' she added, seeing Blair lift an eyebrow at her horrified expression.

'Well, you're still young,' he said indifferently as he made his way round to his door. 'And children are an enormous commitment.'

'Exactly.' Amanda climbed into her seat as well, relieved that he wasn't going to enquire any further into her aversion to children. 'Is that why you don't have any? Because you travel so much?'

Blair turned the ignition key and coaxed the engine into life. 'One of the reasons,' he said uninformatively.

Amanda studied him from under her lashes and wondered what the other reasons were. Why wasn't he married, anyway? Her ready imagination was quick to endow him with a doomed love affair in the past, but when her eye fell on the straight, stern line of his mouth she changed her mind. The Blair McAllisters of this world didn't waste time on desperate romances. They chose wives who were calm and sensible and wouldn't complain about being cold or wet or fed a constant diet of ginger-nuts, she decided glumly.

A strange feeling stirred inside Amanda and she looked away to stare unseeingly at the scenery. Blair wasn't like the other men she had known. He certainly wasn't like Hugh, who had been so handsome and charming and yet, deep down, so stuffy. It was true that Hugh had called the whole thing off in the end, but she really *did* think it had been for the best, no matter how pathetic Blair had made her drunken monologue sound. She wasn't ready to settle down with anyone yet. She wanted to have a good time, not get bogged down in interminable discussions about commitment, which was all her friends ever seemed to do.

It was odd, though, the way she always seemed to attract the kind of men who wanted to get married as soon as they met you. Amanda had learnt to treat them all with light-hearted indifference and to keep at least three men dangling at any one time so that none of them ever had a chance to get serious.

A thought occurred to her as she remembered past boy-friends. She wouldn't want Blair to get the wrong impression. 'Er...what else did I tell you last night?' she asked cautiously.

The grim look dissolved from Blair's face at the trepidation in Amanda's voice. 'Oh, not much,' he said. 'Just about Tim and Rob and Tom and Don and Jim and Ben...'

Amanda's horrified expression had cleared before he was halfway through the list. 'I've never been out with anyone called Ben,' she said wrathfully. '*Or* Tom. And Rob was only—' She caught herself up. 'You just made all those names up!' she accused him.

'Well, I lost track.' Blair shrugged but the glance he sent her was amused. 'You seemed to have such a complicated love life, and they all seemed to have monosyllabic names, but by that time you were halfway down the bottle and it's not surprising I got confused!'

'It's a pity I can't remember anything you told *me* last night,' she said coldly.

'I didn't get a chance to tell you anything,' he said in a dry voice. 'If you want to hear my deepest, darkest secrets, Amanda, you'd better not hog the whisky next time!'

'There won't be a next time.' Amanda folded her arms and looked grumpily out of the window. It was all Blair's fault anyway. If he hadn't forced her to drink his wretched whisky she wouldn't have had the chance to make such a fool of herself, would she? 'After last night, I'm never going to touch whisky again!'

Dundinnie stood on a rocky promontory where sea and loch merged and mingled. The hills dropped down to the water all

around, curving away to the north and to the south in a pur-
plish-blue blur towards the scatter of islands out to sea so that
it was impossible to tell where mainland began and the islands
ended. Amanda felt as if she had come to the edge of the
world. There was nothing here but the wild, interlocking hills
and the water stretching away up the loch and out beyond the
islands.

The bright, early-morning sky had long been swallowed up
by angry, rolling clouds, but as they drove round a bend in
the road that had followed the loch's winding shore the sun
burst through in a dramatic shaft of light and, as if on cue,
pinpointed the castle.

'That's Dundinnie,' said Blair.

From a distance, it was a forbidding-looking building with
bleak, soaring walls, narrow windows and an assortment of
chimneys, turrets and crumbling battlements. Solid and im-
penetrable, it stared gauntly out to sea as if daring anyone to
try and invade it. Those old stones must have seen some terrible battles, Amanda thought. She could practically see the
attackers hurtling themselves at the walls, hear the blood-
curdling screams and the clash and clang of steel. None of it
would have done any good, she was sure. The only way into
Dundinnie would have been by subterfuge. It gave her an odd
feeling to think of herself as merely the latest in a long line
of would-be invaders, but she squashed any guilty qualms. She
had come too far and gone through too much to give up because of a few scruples now!

'It doesn't look exactly cosy,' she said to Blair even as she
wondered what had possessed Norris to think of turning this
bleak castle into a health farm. If she were going to spend a
week drinking water and eating lettuce leaves, she would at
least want to do it in congenial surroundings.

'It's more comfortable than it looks.' Blair's eyes rested on
the castle almost affectionately. 'The exterior is medieval, but

the castle was refurbished in Edwardian times by McAllisters who were nearly as bad at roughing it as you are!'

'That's a relief,' said Amanda, deciding to ignore that particular remark. 'For a nasty moment there I thought I was going to have to throw my slops out into the courtyard and learn to cook on the spit.'

Blair glanced at her and smiled—a swift, unexpected smile that transformed his face and left Amanda, who had given up waiting for it and was quite unprepared, feeling jarred and confused and suddenly breathless. 'We can run to a few more mod cons than that…but there's always the dungeon if your cooking isn't up to scratch!'

Amanda, desperately trying to get her breathing back to normal and to persuade herself that she had imagined that smile, could only hope that he was joking.

She had wanted the chance to have a bath and tidy herself up before she had to face the children, but of course they were already up and having breakfast around a scrubbed table in the vast, vaulted kitchen when Blair showed her in. A pleasant-faced woman with the Highlanders' clear blue eyes and perfect skin turned from the sink to smile at them, but the children were less welcoming. There were two boys, the elder thin and dark with a supercilious expression and the younger chubbier, and a little girl with wide blue eyes and blonde hair tied back in a pony-tail. Blair introduced them as Simon, Nicholas and Emily.

They looked sullenly back at Amanda, who regarded them with equal enthusiasm. They would have been beautiful children had it not been for their sulky faces, she thought. 'Hello,' she said, forcing a bright smile.

'Why is your hair all messy?' asked Emily with a critical look.

Amanda sighed. 'It's a long story.' Her heart sank at their obvious hostility. What if they put horrible things in her bed? She would have to be sweet and understanding, like Julie

Andrews in *The Sound of Music*... At least there weren't seven
of them. She hoped they wouldn't expect her to strum guitars
and make up songs for them. Her singing was even worse than
her cooking.

She glanced under her lashes at Blair, who was explaining
to a placidly unconcerned Maggie why they were late, and
tried to imagine him as Captain Von Trapp. Too rugged, she
decided, and clearly *not* the type to fall in love with the governess. Recollecting herself, she made an effort and smiled at
the children again.

Nicholas and Emily only stared back with dumb insolence,
but Simon pulled a face. A fine Christmas it was promising
to be, Amanda thought glumly. Fed up with them already, she
stuck out her tongue in response. Of course, that *would* be the
moment when Blair turned round and saw her. He frowned.
'I hope you're not going to encourage the children in that kind
of childish behaviour,' he said repressively.

The children sniggered. Amanda shot them a murderous
look. 'I'm not going to do anything until I've had a bath,' she
said coldly.

'You'll be wanting a good wash after the uncomfortable
night you've had,' said Maggie, drying her one good hand on
a teatowel. 'Let me show you to your room.'

At least Maggie was sympathetic, Amanda consoled herself as
she luxuriated in a deep bath. As Blair had promised, the
plumbing was strictly twentieth century; perhaps Norris's
plans for this place weren't quite as idiotic as they had seemed
when she had first caught sight of Dundinnie. They had driven
up into a courtyard where large windows and a huge wooden
door had seemed much more welcoming than the gaunt side
of the castle staring so defiantly out to sea, and her first impressions had been of faded grandeur and an unexpected
warmth.

Reminded of her reasons for being there, Amanda pulled on

narrow black trousers and a pale yellow jumper, and when she had dried her hair back into its usual swinging style and applied some lipstick she felt much more herself. Ready to face Blair McAllister and even those horrible children again, she found her way back down endless stairs and long corridors to the kitchen.

Blair was sitting alone at the table, his hands cupped around a mug of coffee. He had obviously had a bath too, for his dark hair was still damp, and he had changed into a dark blue fisherman's sweater. Unaware of Amanda, who had hesitated in the doorway, he was gazing abstractedly down into his coffee, his expression for once unguarded. On the train, she had worked out from the brief biography that he must be thirty-five, but he had the cool authority of a much older man. Now, sitting in the warm, clean kitchen, he looked for the first time more his age, less watchful, more approachable, slightly troubled.

Amanda wondered what he was thinking about. Unnoticed in the doorway, she rested her clear brown eyes on his face, noting as if for the first time the dark sweep of his lashes and the crisp, exciting line of his cheek, and remembering how he had looked when he had smiled so unexpectedly. His teeth had been white and strong as the smile had creased his cheeks and lit the cool slate eyes with warmth and humour, so that for a moment it had seemed as if she were facing a stranger, but, after all, it had just been a smile. What had there been in that to catch at her heartstrings and send the air whooshing from her lungs? Nothing!

Hardly had she reassured herself than Blair looked up without warning and caught her watching him. Across the room his eyes were keen and very clear against his tanned skin. They held an expression which Amanda couldn't identify but which dried the breath in her throat and left her unable to do more than stand and look helplessly back at him while her

heart began to thump with slow, painful insistence against her
ribs.

For a long, long moment they just stared at each other in a
silence fraught with unspoken tension. Amanda was sure that
Blair could see right through her, that he knew everything
there was to know about her, but when he looked away it was
almost a shock. 'Come and have some coffee,' he said, so
indifferently that she wondered if she had imagined that cu-
rious expression in his eyes. Even so, she felt ridiculously shy
as she crossed the stone-flagged floor to the table and let him
pour some coffee into a mug.

'Where are the children?' she asked, stirring milk into the
coffee and for some reason unable to look at him directly.

'Probably watching television,' said Blair resignedly. 'I suggested you might like breakfast in peace. You can get to know
them later.' He had sent Maggie home, he explained. 'Not that
she was particularly worried when she discovered that we
didn't get in last night as planned. It takes a lot to ruffle
Maggie. She knew that I'd be back as soon as I could, but she
must be tired and I want her to rest that wrist.'

'Does that mean I have to start cooking right away?' asked
Amanda nervously.

'No, there's soup and bread for lunch, and Maggie said
she'd taken a casserole out of the freezer for tonight.'

Good old Maggie! Amanda felt better already. She wasn't
looking forward to humiliating herself in the kitchen, but she
had a naturally buoyant nature and now that she had some
coffee inside her she was even beginning to persuade herself
that the odd effect Blair had on her was due to no more than
a sleepless night—and she *hadn't* slept, no matter what Blair
said!—and an empty stomach.

'I didn't see any other houses,' she said, lavishly buttering
some toast that he had made for her. 'Where has Maggie gone
home *to*?'

'There's a village just round the point. You wouldn't have

seen it as we drove in, but it's only a couple of miles away. Her husband used to own the local garage before he died, and now her son runs it.'

'Perhaps he should look at your car,' suggested Amanda tartly, and Blair gave her a nasty look.

'There's nothing wrong with my car that I can't fix as long as I've got someone of minimum competence to hold the torch!'

Amanda opened her mouth to answer his cutting comment in kind but changed her mind when she saw the look in his eyes, contenting herself with a glare as she reached for the Marmite. 'If Maggie lives in the village, does that mean that you're all on your own here normally?' she said instead with frosty dignity.

'When I'm here,' he said. 'I've spent most of the past few years overseas.' Blair, she noticed, took his coffee strong and black. He probably thought milk was an unnecessary luxury and far too much trouble to take on an expedition. Defiantly, Amanda added more to her own mug, and a spoonful of sugar for good measure.

'Doesn't it get lonely? I wouldn't like to live in a place like this on my own. It must be jam-packed full of ghosts. I bet you can hardly hear yourself think at night for the sound of rattling chains and blood-curdling moans!'

'Fortunately we're not all blessed with your vivid imagination,' said Blair drily. 'I hate to disappoint you, but I've lived here since I was a boy, and I've never encountered a ghost yet.'

If he had, he would probably just have told it to pull itself together, thought Amanda with an inward sigh. 'I still think it must be lonely,' she persisted through a mouthful of toast. 'Haven't you ever thought about having a family just to fill up all those rooms?'

His face closed. 'I'm perfectly happy as I am,' he said with something of a snap. 'Why are you so interested in my domestic arrangements anyway?'

'I'm not interested!' She ruffled up immediately. 'I just wondered why Maggie didn't live here, that's all.'

'Worried about being with me on your own?' Blair asked in a tone which brought a flush to Amanda's cheeks. 'You'll just have to accept the kids as chaperons.'

'I'm sure that won't be necessary,' she said stiffly.

They finished breakfast in silence, huffy on her part and entirely unconcerned on his. Ignoring Amanda, Blair read his way through the previous day's paper, folded it neatly and pushed back his chair. 'I'm going to get on with some work,' he said. 'I suggest you get the children to show you the castle so that you can find your way around, and after that…well, it's up to you. You know more about entertaining children than I do.'

Amanda's idea of entertaining children involved putting them in a room and shutting the door on them, but she supposed that she would have to do a bit more than that if she didn't want to ruin Sue's reputation with the agency for good. Left alone, she finished her coffee, feeling depressed. Her earlier confidence had completely evaporated. What was she doing here, stuck out in the middle of nowhere with three horrible children and a dour, disagreeable Scot who would rather read a paper than talk to her over the breakfast table?

Promotion, that's why she was here. Amanda told herself to think positive. All she had to do was survive Christmas, make a thorough, if surreptitious, report on the state of the castle and maybe, if an opportunity arose, persuade Blair of the advantages of selling. If she managed that, Norris had promised her an executive position within the company, with the prospect of a meteoric rise to the top if she proved her worth. Amanda's slumped shoulders straightened at the thought.

Ambitious but fatally impatient, she had refused to go to

university when she'd had the chance, and instead had launched herself into a series of unsatisfactory jobs, all of which had proved to be short-lived when she'd discovered to her surprise that no one would give an inexperienced nineteen-year-old a position of real responsibility. Amanda had plenty of advantages. She was sharp and witty, tenacious and resourceful, and she had a certain flair that counterbalanced the more extravagant and exuberant side of her character, but, as Sue had pointed out, she didn't quite have the killer instinct that would have ensured her instant success. At vital moments her sense of humour would get the better nof her.

Amanda carried the breakfast dishes over to the sink, still pondering darkly on her frustrated career. Her father had always said that if she was good at her job and stuck at it long enough she would get promoted in the end, but she didn't want to wait that long. She had seen secretaries spend *years* typing memos. Norris Jeffries was the first employer who had offered her real encouragement. He wasn't interested in qualifications or experience, he had said. He was interested in *results*. Amanda had jumped at her chance. She would be a success at last.

And now, here she was, washing dishes in a Scottish castle. Amanda sighed. She just hoped it would be worth it.

CHAPTER FOUR

AMANDA found the children, as Blair had predicted, in front of the television in a cosy sitting room. At least, it was cosy in comparison to the great hall which had a minstrels' gallery, a cavernous fireplace and a lugubrious collection of stuffed deer heads on the walls. In comparison with the flat that she shared with three friends in London, it was vast, but the dark red wallpaper and comfortable, rather shabby sofas gave it a welcoming air.

Nicholas was lying on his stomach but Simon and Emily were lolling over the chairs, apparently too bored even to sit up straight. Amanda fixed on a friendly smile. Sue would say that she should try and understand the problems these children had. 'Hello again,' she said.

They ignored her. Abandoning understanding, Amanda marched over to the television and switched it off. 'I *said* hello,' she repeated dangerously.

'We've already said hello,' muttered Simon rudely.

'Well, now we're saying it again,' she said through clenched teeth. 'Your uncle has suggested that you show me round the castle, if that's not too much effort for you.'

The children exchanged martyred sighs, but it was evident that their rudeness didn't extend as far as disobeying Blair, and they dragged themselves complaining to their feet.

It wasn't long before Amanda was wishing that they hadn't bothered. With a world-weariness quite remarkable in a boy of eleven, Simon trailed around the castle, but since his tour consisted of waving a languid hand and saying, 'Stairs to tower...bedroom...

bedroom…bedroom…stairs…' Amanda didn't find it very informative. It was certainly an extraordinary building with its massive walls, uneven floors and interminable stone spiral staircases. She would have liked to have known more about the history but whenever she asked Simon merely shrugged rudely.

'Dunno.'

Once away from the rooms built around the great hall, Amanda was soon lost, and she began to suspect that the children were deliberately trying to confuse her. The prospect of Christmas with these little monsters was already making her blood run cold. Gritting her teeth, she reminded herself of her prospective promotion.

'This room is haunted.' Nicholas's announcement made little impression on Amanda. She was standing in an empty tower room, staring down through a narrow window at the pebbly beach below and wondering why anyone in their right minds would ever want to have children. 'A nanny got locked in here by mistake and they all thought she'd run away. She starved to death before anyone thought to look in this tower, and when they found her all her fingers were worn to the bone where she'd been trying to open the door.'

Amanda's attention was caught halfway through this charming speech. 'She *what*?' she asked, turning from the window, but by then it was too late. All she saw was Simon slipping through the door before it banged shut. She leapt over to it, only to hear the sinister sound of a bolt being slammed into place.

'Open this door at once!' she shouted, pounding on the door in impotent fury, but her only reply was a stifled giggle and the clatter of footsteps receding down the stone stairs.

They had locked her in.

She tried shouting, of course, but the walls were so thick and they had wandered to such a remote corner of the castle that she knew there was no chance of anyone hearing her.

Even if she could have opened the window, it was a sheer
drop down to the rocks and her voice would have just been
carried away by the wind. Why couldn't Blair live in a
crowded city like everyone else? At this rate she would starve
to death like that other governess. She wouldn't put it beyond
those poisonous children to hide her suitcase and tell him that
she had caught the bus back to Fort William!

Blair let her out an hour and a half later, by which time
Amanda was so angry that she could hardly speak. The tiny
room was completely empty and she had ended up sitting on
the freezing stone floor, convinced that Blair was even now
ringing the agency to complain about her abandoning her post.
The sliding of the bolt as he unlocked the door was the
sweetest sound that she had ever heard, but if she had expected
sympathy from him she was doomed to disappointment.

'I would have thought you would have had some kind of
authority over children,' he said severely, eyeing Amanda with
disapproval as she scrambled to her feet.

'Children? Those aren't children!' she said in a shaking
voice. 'They're the spawn of the devil! They've probably all
got 6-6-6 tattooed on their heads!'

'There's no need to exaggerate,' said Blair irritably. 'It's
not as if they've hurt you.'

'No, they're probably keeping the ritual disembowelment as
a nice little surprise for tonight!'

'Don't be ridiculous!' he snapped, losing his temper. 'If you
can't control them properly, I'll have to ring up the agency
and get them to send somebody else who can.'

It was on the tip of Amanda's tongue to tell him he could
do precisely that, but she remembered Sue's reputation just in
time. And Norris. 'I don't care how you do it,' he had said
before she'd left. 'Just get me what I want and you'll be looking at a rosy future.' He wouldn't think much of her if she

was kicked out of Dundinnie before she had been here a day, would he?

She made a heroic effort to swallow her wrath. 'It always takes children a little time to adjust to someone new,' she managed after a moment, and even produced an insincere smile. 'I'm sure we'll be fine once we all settle down.'

'Make sure you do,' said Blair with a sceptical grunt. 'I can't spare the time to arrange for the agency to send someone else, and frankly I've got better things to do than drive backwards and forwards to Fort William with incompetent nannies!'

Charming! Amanda simmered for the rest of the day, which passed in somewhat tight-lipped silence. In spite of his dismissive attitude to her, Blair had obviously given the children a thundering scold when he'd discovered that she was missing, and equally obviously they were blaming her for it. They treated her with almost threatening formality at mealtimes, but as soon as Blair retreated back into his study they disappeared. That suited Amanda. No doubt they had gone off to plot some revenge attack, but as the day wore on all she cared about was a good night's sleep.

Things were little better the next morning. The temperature had plummeted overnight and on the ground a hard frost glittered in the pale winter sunshine. Blair announced at breakfast that the children were to clean his car as punishment for their treatment of Amanda the day before. The children moaned and groaned, but Amanda noted with satisfaction that Blair ignored their protests, and before they quite knew what had happened they found themselves out in the courtyard equipped with sponges, buckets and a hosepipe. She smirked as she cleared up the breakfast dishes. The sky was already clouding over and it would be very cold out there.

Serve them right, she thought gleefully. When she had cleaned the kitchen and found some more of Maggie's soup for lunch, she went up to the courtyard herself to enjoy their discomfort. 'You've missed a bit here,' she couldn't resist pointing out to Nicholas, who was listlessly wiping a cloth over the number plate.

The look he sent her promised vengeance. Amanda should have been warned by that but when he called out to Simon to chuck him a sponge she didn't even think to step out of the way.

The sponge, icy-cold and dripping water, hit her squarely on the back of the neck. For one horrible moment Amanda could only gasp with shock. 'Sorry!' called Simon insincerely, and Emily and Nicholas giggled.

'Why, you…you…you…' Incapable of words, Amanda snatched up the sponge where it had fallen on the gravel and threw it back in Simon's direction. More by luck than science, it caught him full in the face and he immediately let out a howl of outrage. At that all hell was let loose. Suddenly there were sponges flying in all directions. In no time all the buckets of water had been chucked indiscriminately over everyone, and then Amanda got hold of the hose and turned it on them until Nicholas and Emily managed to wrest it from her and squirt her back.

Somewhere in the middle of all the shrieking and squealing Amanda began to laugh and soon they were all chasing each other round the courtyard, whooping and screaming with laughter, until the children managed to pin her down by the great door to tickle her mercilessly. It was the best fun Amanda had had in ages.

Their mirth was interrupted by the clunk of the huge wooden door opening. Blair stood on the steps, glowering down at the gasping, giggling heap on the gravel. 'What in God's name is going on?' he demanded explosively. His dis-approving gaze fell on Amanda, who disentangled herself from her captors and stood up, her hair wet and dishevelled and her skin glowing from the chase. 'And what do you think *you're* doing?'

'We were just washing the car,' she explained, still trying not to laugh.

'Washing the car? Washing a car doesn't involve making that horrible din, nor does it explain why you are all soaking wet! Look at you!' he went on in disgust. 'You're supposed to be looking after these children, not encouraging them in stupid games.'

He looked so cross that Amanda collapsed back into giggles, which only encouraged the children. 'I'm sorry,' she sighed at last, wiping her eyes.

'I'm glad you find it so amusing,' said Blair in a glacial voice.

'You should be glad that we're having a good time,' she pointed out. 'Shouldn't he?' she added, and looked to the three children for support.

They all nodded vigorously, but far from being gratified by this evidence of a cessation in hostilities Blair only looked more exasperated than ever. 'Well, please go and have a good time somewhere else!' he snapped. 'I'm trying to work. You've got a whole castle to amuse yourself in. Surely it isn't necessary to make that racket right outside my study window? And for God's sake dry those children off,' he ordered Amanda as he turned to go back inside. 'I don't want to have to tell their mother that they've all got pneumonia just in time for Christmas!'

His bad temper did more to unite them than anything else could have done, especially when Amanda sprayed the hose so that it splattered just in front of his feet. The look Blair gave her just before he slammed the door shut made her regret her daring, but when she turned back to the children she saw that they were looking very impressed. Clearly Blair was a somewhat awe-inspiring figure for them. Their clothes, she

saw with a twinge of guilt, were as sodden as hers, but their
small faces were bright for the first time.

'I suppose you *had* better go and put something dry on,'
she said.

'Then what? It's so boring here and it's always raining.'

It had indeed begun to rain again—a steady mizzle that kept
trying to turn itself into snow. Amanda, gathering up the buckets and sponges, thought that Simon might have a point. The
sun only seemed to be able to stay out for ten minutes—just
enough to tantalise with the prospect of a fine day before the
grey clouds came bustling up to cover it like outraged
Victorian matrons spotting an exposed ankle. The clear, frosty
morning had made her feel almost Christmassy, but the rain
was quickly reducing everything to the same depressing shade
of greyish-brown.

'You go and get changed,' she said. 'Then I'll teach you
how to play poker.' It was the only card game she knew apart
from animal snap.

When Blair found them, they were all huddled intently
round the table in the sitting room. Amanda had drawn the
red velvet curtains for atmosphere and a single lamp illumi-
nated the table where she was engaged in a battle of nerves
with Nicholas.

'What's going on in here?' he exploded as he took in the
scene, but they only flapped distracted hands at him.

'Shh!'

Blair was forced to wait in growing impatience until
Nicholas called Amanda's bluff and won with shrieks of excitement. 'I can't believe that you're teaching these children
to gamble!' he accused her as Nicholas scooped up the pile
of matches they had been using instead of money. 'Couldn't
you all be doing something more useful…like getting lunch?'
he added with a dour glance at his watch. 'It's past two
o'clock!'

Amanda was of the opinion that Blair was more than capable of getting his own lunch, but he already looked like a man who was holding onto his temper with difficulty, and she decided that it would be undiplomatic to push him any further that morning.

'Amanda's brilliant at bluffing!' Simon informed his uncle, and Blair's eyebrows took on an even more sarcastic slant than usual.

'That doesn't surprise me in the least!'

Amanda tilted her chin at him as she swept the cards together. 'I'll go and get the lunch,' she said with dignity.

Somewhat to her surprise, the children clattered down to the kitchen with her. 'You're not at all like the nannies we usually have,' said Simon with the air of one delivering a great compliment.

She glanced over her shoulder to check whether Blair was within earshot and then beckoned them closer, laying a finger across her lips. 'Can you keep a secret?'

Three heads nodded in unison. 'I'm not a real nanny,' she confided with a straight face. 'I'm a secret agent, sent to infiltrate Dundinnie Castle.' Their eyes widened into saucers although Simon clearly thought he ought to retain a certain cynicism.

'Does Uncle Blair know?'

'No, and he mustn't suspect,' said Amanda, rather enjoying casting Blair into a villain's role. 'He's got to go on thinking that I'm a bit silly, so that I can stay here and find out as much about the castle as I can without him knowing.'

'But why?' gasped Emily, enthralled.

Good question. Amanda assumed a considering expression while she thought of an answer. 'Let's just say that we suspect something very fishy has been going on here,' she said darkly at last, hoping that they wouldn't ask who 'we' were.

'Can we help?'

'You can help me draw a plan of the castle,' she said, spotting the perfect excuse to poke around and entertain the chil-

dren at the same time. With any luck, they'd end up doing all
the work for her and she would be able to produce an even
more detailed report for Norris than she had dreamt.

It certainly kept them happy all afternoon, rushing around
with measuring tapes and pencils and bits of paper. 'What are
they doing?' Blair asked Amanda as he crossed the great hall
on his way back to his study and watched Emily and Nicholas
disappear busily up the stairs. 'They're very quiet.'

'Oh, just a project,' said Amanda airily.

'A project?' He fixed her with a sceptical look. 'What sort
of project?'

'A secret one,' she said.

'Hmm,' grunted Blair, turning to his study. He paused with
his hand at the door and looked back at Amanda who was
looking suspiciously innocent as she headed towards the sitting room where she had every intention of spending the afternoon with a magazine. His expression was half puzzlement,
half grudging admiration. 'It looks as if you know how to deal
with children after all,' he said with evident reluctance. 'I was
beginning to wonder if you were really a nanny at all!'

Amanda disposed herself on a sofa and congratulated herself
on having arranged everything perfectly. Perhaps Christmas
wouldn't be so bad after all. The children were occupied, she
had made a start on getting the information for Norris and
even Blair had changed his opinion of her.

If he had, he had changed it back again by that evening.
Supper was a disaster, for a start. Having forgotten to take one
of Maggie's dishes out of the freezer, Amanda was reduced
to cooking herself. There was no microwave, only a huge Aga,
and no handy packets with instructions on the back, and the
best she could manage was to undercook some pasta and over-
cook some vegetables into a mush for a sauce. She always
enjoyed it when friends made it for her, but it didn't taste the
same when she did it. The children pushed it round their plates

and she found it hard to whip up any enthusiasm for it herself. Blair ate his way stolidly through his plateful, but she knew that he was mentally reviewing what the agency had told him about her supposed cooking skills.

'It always takes a little time to get used to a new kitchen,' she said to forestall any comment.

'I hope you're going to get used to it in time for Christmas,' grunted Blair, and Amanda looked at him with foreboding.

'Maggie's wrist will be better by then, won't it?'

'Probably, but she will naturally spend Christmas with her own family. I've no intention of asking her to come here just because you can't cope with cooking the turkey.'

Amanda lay down her fork. She hadn't given much thought to Christmas itself, but now for the first time the reality of the situation hit her. 'You mean it'll just be us?'

'I thought I'd explained that to the agency,' said Blair irritably. 'Since Belinda can't be here, someone needs to make Christmas special for the children.'

'I see.' Amanda tried to look cheerful and competent, the kind of person who could produce mince pies and Christmas pudding at the drop of a hat. 'Well—er—what do you usually do here at Christmas? There must be some Dundinnie traditions, aren't there?'

'I haven't spent Christmas here for years,' said Blair. 'Not since...not for a long time.' His expression was oddly shuttered. 'You do whatever you think best.'

'What about you?' Amanda turned to the children. 'What's Christmas like at home?'

'It was awful last year,' muttered Simon. 'It was our first Christmas without Dad and Mum cried a lot.'

Amanda made haste to retreat from what was obviously dangerous ground. 'In that case, we'll have to make up our own traditions, won't we?' she said brightly. 'I know, let's agree not to have any presents...'

'Oh, no!' cried Emily and Nicholas simultaneously, and

even Blair grinned at their appalled expressions. He looked quite different when he smiled. It was like blinking and finding that someone you knew had suddenly turned into a perfect stranger—someone younger and warmer and infinitely more disturbing. Amanda had to jerk her eyes away and concentrate fiercely on breathing past the odd, tight feeling in her chest.

'All right,' she said, throwing up her hands in mock surrender and wondering if Blair noticed how strange her voice sounded. 'We'll make it a real, traditional Christmas Day instead. What shall we do first?'

'Open our stockings,' said Emily, not yet entirely reassured that Amanda had been joking when she'd suggested abandoning the idea of presents.

'Stockings first,' agreed Amanda, 'and then champagne for breakfast.'

'For breakfast?' Blair lifted a disapproving eyebrow.

'Why not?' She met his gaze challengingly. 'It is Christmas, after all, and you said we could do whatever I thought best.'

'Hmm,' said Blair, clearly already regretting his words.

'Can we have some?' asked Simon.

'Certainly,' said Amanda as Blair opened his mouth to say no. 'A taste, anyway,' she amended.

'What then?' said Emily eagerly, and Amanda, remembering Christmases from her own childhood, could feel her enthusiasm gathering.

'Well, we'll go to church in the morning and then come back and open our presents, with another bottle of champagne,' she suggested provocatively, casting a naughty look at Blair. 'Then…let's see…lunch, of course, and perhaps it'll be snowing and afterwards we can build a snowman, and then we'll come back and have tea by the fire and pick the marzipan off the Christmas cake.' Carried away by her own ideas, she rested her elbows on the table and beamed at the children, who had brightened at the mention of presents, anyway. 'And we'll sing carols and decorate the castle with holly and mistletoe—it'll be wonderful!'

Nicholas had been listening carefully, but now a thought suddenly struck him. 'Why do you always have to have holly and mistletoe?' he asked curiously.

'Well, the holly because it looks so nice at Christmas, I suppose,' said Amanda. 'And you have to have mistletoe! You can kiss anyone standing under the mistletoe.'

Predictably Simon and Nicholas screwed up their faces. 'Yuk! I'm not going to do that!'

'That's not very nice!' Amanda laughed, trying to look offended. 'What am I going to do if you two won't kiss me?'

'You can kiss Uncle Blair,' Emily offered kindly. 'Can't she, Uncle Blair?'

There was a tiny pause. 'I'm sure a girl like Amanda won't have any trouble finding someone to kiss her,' said Blair in a dry voice, and to her horror Amanda felt a wave of hot colour surge up her cheeks.

She got up hastily and began clearing away the plates, furious with Blair for sounding so cool about the whole idea, furious with Emily for even suggesting it, furious with herself for not being able to dismiss the whole thing out of hand. The trouble was that once the idea of kissing Blair had presented itself she couldn't dislodge it. It appalled her to realise that she didn't need to look at his mouth to picture it with unnerving clarity. She knew just what it was like when it was drawn disapprovingly down at the corners, when it twisted with exasperated amusement, or when it relaxed into one of those rare, unsettling smiles.

Washing dishes mindlessly, Amanda suddenly found herself remembering how Pippa had described Blair as gorgeous. He wasn't, she decided. Not really. It would just be nice if he smiled at her more often, that was all.

It would be even nicer if she didn't feel so ridiculously nervous about spending the evening alone with him. Last

night, shattered by the journey, she had retired at the same
time as the children, but she couldn't do that tonight. It would
be the first time that she and Blair had been alone since they
had shared breakfast yesterday, she realised, and she remembered his comment about having to make do with the children
as chaperons.

Not that she would have any need of a chaperon. Blair had
made it very clear that he had no interest in her. Still, the
thought of being alone with him made Amanda unaccountably
nervous and she wished fiercely that Emily had never said
anything about a kiss.

Irritably, she wiped her hands on a teatowel and took herself
to task. It wasn't as if she were some Victorian maiden. She
had spent evenings alone with lots of men, most of them a lot
more charming than Blair McAllister, and she had never felt
in the slightest bit awkward. She had always been the sort of
person who could be guaranteed to get a party going, or fill a
difficult silence with a funny story, and there was absolutely
no reason for butterflies to start flapping around inside her at
the idea of sitting opposite Blair and trying not to look at his
mouth. She would take a good book and sit in an armchair,
and after waiting an hour or so, just to show how unconcerned
she was, she would excuse herself and go to bed. What was
so nerve-racking about that?

'Nothing,' said Amanda out loud to the fire as she waited
for Blair to come down after saying goodnight to the children.
'Absolutely nothing.' But it didn't stop her heart turning a
peculiar somersault when the door opened and he came in.

Why did it *do* that? It wasn't even as if he were particularly
handsome. All right, he had an unnervingly attractive smile,
but he didn't use it very often, and he certainly wasn't smiling
now. In fact, he looked distinctly cross.

'What's this ridiculous story you've been telling Emily
about being a spy?' he demanded as he poured himself a drink.

'Well, she's not much good at keeping a secret, is she?' exclaimed Amanda in involuntary indignation.

Blair's mouth drew down at the corners. 'She's only seven, and was obviously bursting to tell me. She seemed to think it might improve you in my eyes.' He snorted at the idea. 'Apparently I've got to go on thinking that you're rather silly... and I shouldn't find *that* too difficult!'

'I was just teasing,' she said rather sulkily. 'It's much more fun for them to think of me as a secret agent than as a boring old nanny.'

Blair stared at her with a mixture of incredulity and disapproval. 'You seem to have the most extraordinary ideas about how to deal with children!'

'I didn't notice you complaining when they were quiet this afternoon,' snapped Amanda, who was secretly relieved to find Blair disagreeable once more. It made it much easier to forget how awkward she had been feeling just before he'd come in. Defensively, she tucked her legs up beneath her on the chair. 'Anyway, if you know so much about dealing with children, why don't you deal with them yourself?'

'Because I'm paying you a vast sum of money to do it for me,' he reminded her coldly. 'I hope that you'll start earning your money tomorrow by doing something useful with them. So far their activities have been limited to gambling and tomfoolery with hosepipes!' Crossing over to the fire, he threw himself down into the armchair opposite Amanda's and regarded her with a kind of baffled exasperation. 'I can't think what the agency were talking about when they told me that you were a nice, quiet girl! Dundinnie was a peaceful place until you came along.'

She gaped at him. 'But I haven't done anything!'

Blair continued to eye her moodily over the rim of his glass. 'You haven't done anything you're supposed to do, no,' he agreed. 'I wanted someone steady who would cook and clean and establish a quiet routine for the children, and what do I get? A drama queen of the first order!'

'I am *not*!' Amanda protested hotly, stung by the accusation. It wasn't the first time it had been levelled against her, it had to be admitted, but that didn't make it any easier to bear.

'Yes, you are,' he corrected her. 'I've never met anyone so prone to exaggeration! One minute you and the children are at each other's throats, and the next you've roped them into one of your absurd fantasies!'

'I thought you wanted us to get on?'

'Why can't you get on *quietly*, like everyone else?' Blair swirled the whisky irritably around his glass and glared into the fire. 'You're so...extreme about everything. I can't concentrate on my book for wondering what you're doing next.'

Amanda folded her arms huffily across her chest. 'It's not my fault if you're a repressed Scot,' she said unwisely, and his head jerked round to fix her with an unnervingly direct stare.

'What exactly do you mean by that?'

She had said too much to back down now, so she stuck out her chin instead in defiance at his expression. 'You just hate the thought of anyone having a good time!' she accused him. 'God knows what Christmas is going to be like! You nearly had apoplexy at the thought of champagne on Christmas Day, didn't you?'

'I certainly thought that two bottles between the two of us before lunch sounded rather excessive,' said Blair repressively.

'I wasn't really suggesting that we get plastered!' Amanda sighed. Ostentatiously, she picked up a magazine that lay on the floor. 'I was just trying to think of ways to make the day special, as *you* asked me to, if you remember! I should have known that it would take more than a few glasses of champagne to warm you up!'

Blair regarded her with dislike. 'This wouldn't have anything to do with the fact that I didn't jump at the idea of kissing you under the mistletoe, would it?' he enquired sardonically.

'Don't be ridiculous!' Amanda pressed her lips together and turned a page of the magazine with studied insolence. 'I can assure you that I dislike the idea quite as much as you do!'

Blair didn't even deign to reply and she glowered unseeingly down at the page. That was typical! Dare to point out his lack of enthusiasm and suddenly it was all *her* problem! She flicked over another page so savagely that the paper tore. So he thought she wanted him to kiss her, did he? How arrogant could you get? Blair was the *last* man she would want to bump into under the mistletoe. She liked her men to be romantic and charming and fun, none of which applied to Blair McAllister. Realising that she was reading an article on the joys of motherhood, Amanda scowled and moved on.

'Assertiveness in the office': this was more like her. She tried to concentrate but the words just blurred in front of her eyes, and she was far more aware of Blair who was drinking his whisky and looking into the fire, apparently unconcerned by the way she was determinedly ignoring him. When she thought he wasn't looking, Amanda risked a quick glance at him. His expression was guarded, absorbed, and she wondered what he was thinking about. Not about her, that was for sure.

She suppressed a sigh. Why should she care anyway? He was rude, prejudiced, intolerant, generally insufferable. So why, instead of reading, was she wondering what it would be like if he were the kind of man who *would* kiss her under the mistletoe? What would it be like if he really did want to make love to her, if all she had to do was look up and smile? Then she found herself remembering how he had undone the buttons on her shirt in the darkness, and deep inside her something warm and disturbing stirred, while her pulse began to boom in her ears.

Desperately, she turned another page. The rustle of paper sounded very loud in the brittle silence, which was broken only by the spluttering of the burning logs. 'Ten Top Tips To Improve Your Sex Life.' Half-fascinated, half-appalled, Amanda glanced down the list. If Blair had been anyone else, she would have read out excerpts of the article and they would have laughed.

But Blair wasn't anyone else, and the tension between them was bad enough already without introducing a discussion about sex. Even so, having started to think about it, she couldn't stop. She couldn't stop imagining what he would be like as a lover, how that stern mouth would relax into a smile and then a kiss, how sure his hands would be against her skin. A long shiver snaked its way down Amanda's spine.

Amanda realised that she was staring rigidly at the magazine and drew in her breath with a tiny gasp. It was enough to make Blair glance up from the fire, suddenly alert.

'What's the matter?'

'Nothing.' Her voice sounded high and thin and she cleared her throat hurriedly. 'Nothing.'

He looked at her curiously for a moment and then turned back to the fire. With an enormous effort, Amanda forced her eyes to focus on the page. Oh, God, she was still on 'Ten Top Tips...' 'Talk to each other,' she read. 'Your partner can't be expected to know what you like unless you tell him. Don't be afraid to confide your secret fantasies—you might both be surprised at the results!'

Amanda tried to envisage herself making a confession: Blair, I keep thinking about how you undressed me in the dark car. Surprise would be an inadequate way to describe his probable reaction! At the thought of Blair's face in such a situation, a bubble of hysterical laughter rose up inside her, and she was so taken up with suppressing it that she didn't notice that he had got to his feet until he leant down to the wood basket just by her armchair.

Unprepared for his sudden movement, Amanda jerked back in her chair with an exclamation of surprise and slammed the magazine shut before he could see what she had been reading. Blair froze in the middle of straightening with a log in his hand and stared down at her.

'*Now* what is it?'

'Nothing,' she said again in a strangled voice.

'I'm just putting some more wood on the fire,' he went on, very distinctly, dropping the log on the fire and bending down for another one. 'You don't have any objection, I take it?'

'No. Absolutely not. Good idea.' She spoke heartily but her eyes slid away from Blair's as he stood over her, brushing the sawdust thoughtfully from his hands.

'You seem very nervous, Amanda,' he said at last, his voice cool and faintly mocking.

'Nervous?' She tried a laugh but it was a mistake. 'What have I got to be nervous about?'

'That's just what I'm asking myself,' said Blair slowly. 'And since the answer is *nothing*, I can only assume that vivid imagination of yours is working overtime as usual.'

Amanda fumbled for the magazine which had slid down the side of the chair. 'I don't know what you mean.'

'Don't you?' He bent down without warning and placed his hands on either arm of her chair so that she was effectively penned in. 'I thought that with your sense of drama you would have been anticipating a passionate seduction scene tonight at the very least!' For a long moment he looked down at Amanda where she sat curled in the old armchair, the firelight gleaming on her glossy brown hair and her eyes huge and abruptly apprehensive, and then he reached for her wrists and without haste pulled her to her feet in front of him.

Amanda went unresistingly. She felt boneless, weak, incapable of protest. The strong fingers around her wrists seemed to be all that were holding her upright, and when Blair released them to slide his hands up her arms it was all she could do not to sway towards him for support. 'Did you think that I would try to take advantage of you, Amanda?' he asked, the mockery in his voice overlaid by a newer, less recognisable undercurrent. 'Were you waiting for me to discover whether you're as soft and warm and vibrant as you look?'

His hands burned through her shirt as they slid slowly but surely up to her shoulders. Amanda couldn't move, couldn't speak. She knew that she could step sideways out of his reach. She even knew that that was what she *ought* to do, but the slate-grey eyes looking down into hers held her immobile and all she could do was stare hopelessly back up at him while his voice reverberated down through his hands and over her skin, evaporating the air in her lungs and making her heart lurch unsteadily around her chest. She was caught in a web of awareness that tightened around her as his hands drifted tantalisingly along her jaw to tangle in her shining hair.

'D-don't be ridiculous,' she managed to croak as he let her hair spill through his fingers.

'It's not any more ridiculous than any of your other stories, is it?' said Blair softly, and she closed her eyes as he tilted her face between his hands, bending his head until his lips were almost, but not quite, touching hers. 'Is this what was making you so twitchy, Amanda? Were you waiting for me to kiss you?' he murmured, and hesitated just long enough for Amanda to open her eyes and wonder with a pang if he had decided not to kiss her after all. Blair read the confusion in her face and smiled wickedly. 'Like this?' he said, and brought his mouth down onto hers at last.

CHAPTER FIVE

FOR Amanda, it was as if time itself had stopped. The touch of his lips was like stepping out into an abyss, and she was left spinning above a terrifying swirl of uncharted sensation; Blair's palms against her face were all that was holding her above a dizzying fall.

Amanda had never felt that mixture of panic and blind, breathless exhilaration before. Her first reaction was to clutch onto him as her one contact with reality, and when Blair relaxed his hold she half murmured in protest and curled her fingers convulsively into the rough wool of his jumper. So confused was she that it was even a relief to discover that he had let her go only to gather her hard against him and deepen the kiss.

All that time she had spent thinking about his mouth, and still she hadn't dreamt how warm it would be, how persuasive. How could she have guessed how insistently it would explore her own, or how the pressure of those firm lips would melt any resistance and elicit in response feelings that Amanda hadn't even known she possessed?

The shivery excitement of his kiss was intoxicating, irresistible, and all she could do was cling to him, bewildered by the rush of conflicting emotions. She was totally unprepared, almost frightened by the giddy sensations his touch had unleashed. Half of her wanted him to stop, to let her grasp back her fragile control. The other half recognised an inexplicable sense of belonging, as if his arms were a shelter and the hard strength of his body a security, and that some deep, hitherto unacknowledged part of her wanted him to hold her close like this for ever.

She never knew how long that devastating kiss lasted. It seemed to take on a power of its own, generating an electric excitement that spiralled dangerously towards the limits of control and for which she was sure Blair was almost as unprepared as she was. It was he who broke it, though, lifting his head with a tangible effort. His hold on her slackened and his lips left hers almost reluctantly.

'You see, we didn't need the mistletoe after all.' His voice was a little ragged, but he had himself well under control.

His words slammed the brakes on the still spinning pleasure of his kiss and Amanda was jolted sickeningly back to reality, gasping with shock as if she had been thrown violently off a roundabout.

'What...?' She drew a shuddering breath and steadied her voice with difficulty. 'What did you do that for?'

'It seems to me that you have an alarming tendency to confuse fantasy and reality,' said Blair. 'I just thought it was time you learnt to distinguish between the two.'

Amanda found herself thinking about how she had sat watching him from under her lashes and in spite of herself a great wave of colour swept into her face. 'I'm quite aware of the difference,' she said shakily. 'And even if I hadn't been, was there any need to make your point quite so drastically?'

'Well, I enjoyed it,' said Blair. He looked down at his chest where her fingers were still gripping his jumper. 'Didn't you?'

Awash with humiliation, she jerked her hands away. 'No, I didn't!' she whispered, but she knew that she lied.

Blair knew it too.

Somehow she got herself out of the room and up the stairs on legs that still trembled. She had been kissed plenty of times before, but never with such shattering effect, and she was appalled by her own response. How could she have succumbed so easily? She hadn't even *tried* to push him away! The merest touch of his hands and she had been lost. It was pathetic!

Burning with humiliation, Amanda lay on her bed. She felt

hot and feverish, and her body twitched with what she refused to admit was unsatisfied desire. She told herself that she would die rather than let Blair lay a finger on her again, but, no matter how hard she tried, she couldn't forget the wild, rocketing excitement or how strong and solid his body had been. She had been desperate to be on her own, but now that she was she was conscious of a quite ridiculous sense of loss.

If Blair had been kissing her because he loved her, she wouldn't be lying there restless and alone. He would be stretching out beside her, smoothing his hands over her skin with a smile...

'Stop it! Stop it!' Amanda thrust the image away and threw herself over onto her other side. She hated the way Blair made her feel. *She* liked to be the one in control! She didn't want to spend the next month thinking about his mouth or his hands or the way he looked when he smiled. She wanted to go back to being the way she normally was—confident and capable and not the kind of girl who wasted her time thinking about a man who had made no secret of the fact that he disliked her.

At breakfast the next morning, she was coldly dignified. She had no intention of letting Blair guess what effect his kiss had had on her. After his comments about her extreme behaviour, she knew that he would be expecting her to make a scene, but she was determined to make him admit that he had been wrong about her. If he was waiting for her to demand an apology or an explanation, he was doomed to disappointment. No, she would be cool, crisp and composed, and Blair would be at first baffled by her transformation then thoroughly ashamed of himself.

That was the idea, anyway. Unfortunately, Blair showed no sign of noticing any difference in her at all. He read through the paper in taciturn silence just as he had done every morning so far, and ignored both her and the children.

Amanda eyed him in frustration. *He* hadn't been awake half

the night practising how to be cool; it came naturally to him, but it was a real effort for her to maintain a chilly silence and he might at least have the decency to appreciate it! She stirred her coffee belligerently, clinking the spoon against the side of the cup, but even that didn't irritate him enough to make him look up.

'I thought I'd go and see how Maggie is,' she said distantly, forced in the end to speak first. Actually, she wanted Maggie's advice about cooking so that she could impress Blair with some dazzling meal that would show him that she wasn't the incompetent he thought her, but she saw no need to tell *him* that. 'Can I take the car?'

At last, a reaction! Blair lowered the paper. 'You're just going to the village?'

'Yes.'

'Had it occurred to you that you might walk?'

His sarcastic tone made her lips tighten. 'It's raining,' she pointed out frostily.

Blair folded his paper and dropped it onto the table as he got to his feet. 'A bit of rain won't kill you,' he said. 'You can borrow a jacket and there are a whole lot of boots out in the boiler room.'

At least the walk worked off some of her ill-humour. Rather to Amanda's surprise, Emily had opted to accompany her in spite of the rain, and by the time they had grumbled about Blair's disagreeableness in making them get wet, the rain which had been trying to turn itself into snow had given up and stopped anyway, leaving the sky a cold, blank grey.

Maggie was delighted to see them both and dug out a couple of cookery books for Amanda to consult while Emily played with the neighbour's kittens. 'I wish I could do more to help,' she said as Amanda made them both a cup of coffee. 'I can't be doing with sitting around all day, but Blair insisted that I rest until my wrist is completely better and it would be more than my life's worth to go back before then!'

'He's very autocratic, isn't he?' complained Amanda, carrying the cups across to the kitchen table, where Maggie was sitting with her wrist still heavily strapped. 'He seems to spend his whole time ordering people around. It must be hell to be on expedition with him!'

'Oh, that's just his way,' said Maggie comfortably. 'There's no one I'd rather be with in a difficult situation, and that's a fact. Blair keeps things to himself, but you wouldn't find a better friend if you needed one. When my Jim died, I don't know what we'd have done without him. If it hadn't been for him, Alan—that's my son—would never have been able to keep the garage going, and it's not as if Blair has much money himself.'

'He must make a bit with all those books and television programmes, though,' said Amanda, unwilling to see Blair cast in such a heroic light.

'Well, yes, but it's nothing compared to the upkeep on a place like Dundinnie. And the death duties!' Maggie shook her head. 'He never expected to inherit Dundinnie, you know, but first his cousin died and then his uncle... that was a terrible business! Terrible!'

'Why? What happened?'

'Malcolm was killed in a car crash and I think his poor father just died of grief,' sighed Maggie. 'Malcolm was such a lovely boy,' she added sadly. 'They were all lovely. Malcolm, Blair and Belinda... it's so sad to think that none of them found much happiness. Here's Malcolm dead all these years and Belinda divorced.'

Amanda forced her voice to sound casual. 'What about Blair? He hasn't been married, has he?'

'No.' The housekeeper sighed again. 'He was engaged once... oh, over ten years ago now. I remember he brought her up here. Iona, her name was,' she said. 'She was a beautiful girl—long auburn hair and green eyes—and Blair was so in love with her.' Amanda's fingers had tightened around her cup but Maggie didn't notice. 'I don't know what happened. I just heard that it had all fallen through and then Blair went off to Africa and it was nearly three years before he came home again.' She shook her head sadly again. 'I've never heard him mention her since, but he's never brought anyone else up here.'

Amanda put her cup carefully down in her saucer and told herself that she didn't feel in the slightest bit jealous at the idea of Blair being in love with the beautiful Iona. She would have known what it was like to be kissed by him too, only Blair wouldn't have kissed Iona the way he had kissed *her* last night. He wouldn't have let Iona go. Iona wouldn't have had to spend the night tossing and turning in a lonely bed.

'Are you all right, dear?' Maggie peered at Amanda in concern. 'You look a bit odd.'

Amanda flashed her a brittle smile. 'I'm fine, Maggie. Absolutely fine.' She pushed back her chair, deciding that she didn't want to hear any more about the beautiful Iona. 'I think Emily and I should be getting back.'

Emily had to be lured away from the kitten by the promise of sweets from the tiny village post office. 'Uncle Blair only lets us have sweets on special occasions,' she told Amanda doubtfully as they waved goodbye to Maggie.

'Well, *I'm* letting you have sweets now,' said Amanda, who was still feeling unaccountably cross at the idea of Blair having been in love with anyone called Iona...*Iona*—of all the stupid, pretentious names! What could you expect of someone with red hair and green eyes, though? 'We've had to walk all the way down here in the rain. A sweet is the least we deserve!'

Thrilled with her unexpected treat, Emily spent so long choosing which sweets to have that Amanda's mind began to wander. Why had Blair's engagement to Iona fallen through? Had he broken it off or had she? He didn't seem like the kind of man who would change his mind, but it was hard to imagine any girl giving him up either. Of course, Blair would have been much younger then, only twenty-four or five, but Amanda didn't think he would have changed that much. Perhaps Iona discovered just how grumpy he was in the mornings? Only he probably wouldn't have *been* grumpy with her, Amanda reminded herself. Iona wouldn't have had to trudge for miles in the pouring rain!

Emily's choice was made at last, and Amanda headed for the door, but she was so wrapped in her thoughts that she walked right into a man who had just come in. 'Oh, I'm so sorry!' she apologised, and found herself looking up at an open, smiling face.

'Don't apologise!' he said with an appreciative grin. 'It was a pleasure!'

'I wasn't looking where I was going, I'm afraid.'

'I should have got out of your way,' he said gallantly. 'It was obvious that you were miles away. What were you thinking about?'

Blair's image shimmered in Amanda's mind and she thrust it angrily away. 'Nothing important,' she said firmly.

'That's a pity. I was rather hoping you might need to tell the doctor all about it.' He stuck out his hand. 'Dr Iain Ferguson...but Iain to you since you're obviously not in need of my professional services!'

He was a big man with reddish-gold hair and bright blue eyes. He had a solid, dependable air and an engaging smile that made him instantly likeable. Amanda smiled as she shook his hand and introduced herself in return. 'And this is Emily.'

'So you're staying at the castle?' said Iain when she had explained what they were doing in the village. 'Does that mean Blair McAllister's in residence?' he added eagerly.

'Unfortunately,' said Amanda with something of a snap. 'I suppose you know him?'

'No, but I've been looking forward to meeting him. I've read all his books, of course, but I only moved here a month or so ago, and he doesn't seem the type to need a doctor very often. I was rather hoping I might bump into him,' he went on with disarming candour, 'but he obviously keeps himself to himself when he's up here.'

'He's trying to finish a book at the moment,' said Amanda. 'That's why I'm here.' She explained that the children were staying with Blair while their mother was in New Zealand. 'I'm here to look after you, aren't I?' she added, tugging Emily's pony-tail gently. The little girl was clutching her bag of sweets and staring up at Iain with a dazzled expression.

'You look a very unlikely nanny,' said Iain with an admiring look. 'How long are you here for?'

'About a month...just until Belinda gets back.'

'You'll practically be a local by the time you leave. Look,' he went on impulsively, 'I know it's a bit of cheek, but you wouldn't like to go out to dinner one night, would you? I don't often meet anyone new, so I have to take my opportunities!' He nodded over to the counter and grinned. 'I'm sure Mrs Currie here will vouch for me.'

'I'm not sure what the position is about me taking an evening off,' said Amanda doubtfully, but already the prospect of a meal cooked by someone else was appealing, and besides, it wouldn't do Blair any harm to see that other people appreciated her company, even if he didn't! 'But if Blair says it's OK, I'd love to come.'

Iain's face lit up. 'Great!'

Outside, the rain was trying to snow again, with rather more success this time. Amanda peered out at the first few flakes splattered on the cars and grimaced. 'I think we'd better be getting back, Emily.'

'If you hang on while I get some milk, I'll give you a lift back,' Iain offered promptly. 'I'm going that way anyway.'

Amanda and Emily accepted with alacrity as the sleet gathered energy. As he drove them back along the lochside, Iain told them about his practice and how different it was from his previous one in Edinburgh.

'What made you come here?' Amanda asked curiously.

'I wanted a change,' he said. 'I went through rather a nasty divorce last year, and it seemed a good idea to make a complete break and start afresh somewhere different. It does get lonely sometimes, but it's beautiful country, and you never know who you're going to meet in the post office!'

He drove right into the courtyard so that they wouldn't get too wet. 'You won't forget about dinner, will you?' he said boyishly, and handed Amanda a card with his telephone number on it.

'I'll ring you as soon as I've found out when I can get an evening off,' she promised. 'Thanks for the lift, Iain.'

Taking Emily's hand, she dashed through the sleet, turning in the shelter of the great doorway to wave goodbye before pushing open the heavy wooden door.

'Who was that?' Blair appeared so suddenly that Amanda jumped guiltily. She had forgotten that his study looked out over the drive.

'Amanda's got a boyfriend,' announced Emily pertly, and Blair's black brows snapped together.

'Don't be silly, Emily!' Amanda put in quickly before he could speak. She felt unaccountably flustered, but met Blair's hard stare as coolly as she could. 'As a matter of fact, that was the new doctor, Iain Ferguson. We met him in the post office and he kindly gave us a lift home.'

'Amanda's going to have dinner with him,' added Emily, who was dazzled by what she perceived as Amanda's new conquest.

Blair looked grim. 'Oh, she is, is she?'

'Emily, why don't you go and find out what the boys are doing?' said Amanda hurriedly. 'You can give them their share of the sweets we bought.'

'Do you make it a practice to accept lifts from strange

men?' demanded Blair as Emily trailed reluctantly off. 'Hardly
a good example to set Emily! And what's this about sweets?'
he added, belatedly registering her last words. 'They're only
allowed sweets on special occasions.'

'A few sweets aren't going to kill them,' snapped Amanda,
not sorry to divert the argument. 'It must be bad enough for
them as it is, being stuck up in the middle of nowhere with a
grumpy uncle. I think they deserve a few treats.'

'I'm not paying you to think,' said Blair unpleasantly. 'Nor
am I paying you to teach Emily how to pick up the first stray
man that crosses her path!'

Amanda gasped in indignation. 'I did not pick Iain up!'

'Oh, it's Iain already, is it?' he sneered. 'It didn't take you
long to get on first-name terms!'

'That's because I thought we were living in the twentieth
century,' she flashed back. 'Silly of me! You should have told
me that nineteenth-century rules still applied at Dundinnie and
I wouldn't have been so shockingly forward in calling you
Blair—and me a servant too!' She assumed a cowed expression. 'From now on I'll remember to call you Mr McAllister.
Or would you prefer sir—or master, perhaps?'

Blair glowered. 'Don't be ridiculous! The situation's entirely different. You're living in my home, so of course I don't
expect you to treat me formally, but you don't even know this
man.'

'I know he's a doctor and therefore presumably respectable
enough even for you. I know he's friendly and unassuming
and kind enough to be concerned that Emily and I didn't have
to walk through the snow—which is more than I can say for
you!'

'He sounds like your ideal man,' Blair agreed with a sat-
urnine expression. 'Amenable enough to let himself be whee-
dled into a dinner invitation before he'd known you five
minutes! Did you tell him how lucky he was to meet you up

here, instead of in London where he'd have had to join a very long queue?'

Amanda set her teeth. 'Dinner was Iain's idea,' she said grittily. 'I said I'd have to check with you first.'

'Well, if this is you checking, the answer's no!'

'I don't see what you can possibly object to,' she said, still through clenched teeth. 'Unless, that is, you're afraid I might end up with someone who isn't a real gentleman—the sort of man who would take advantage of me and kiss me against my will, for instance?'

Blair's reaction to her gibe was to take her chin in the steel grip of one hand. 'I can't believe that anyone could make you do anything against your will, Amanda,' he said, his cold blue-grey eyes boring down into her stormy face. 'You're too used to getting your own way.'

'I didn't get my own way last night,' she said bravely, even though her spine shivered at the pressure of his fingers.

His mouth twisted and his hand fell from her face. 'Didn't you?'

'Of course I didn't! You didn't really think I wanted you to kiss me, did you?' Amanda rubbed her chin and hoped she sounded suitably incredulous. It didn't do to remember too much about what she had been thinking just before that shattering kiss.

'I think you enjoyed it, whether you wanted to or not,' said Blair. 'But if you were planning to repeat the experience with your medical friend you can think again. You're not here for a social life, so you can just ring up and cancel whatever arrangements you've made.'

'I'm entitled to some time off!' Amanda protested indignantly, but he was unimpressed.

'Not yet, you're not,' he said, getting ready to slam back into his study. 'You've only been here three days and you haven't even started to earn your salary. You're going to have to do a little more work and little less disrupting of the children's routine before you get a night off!'

It was snowing again. Amanda stared out through the window and wondered whether Norris had considered the depressing effect of the weather on his guests. The snow had been exciting at first, but away from the blazing fires the castle was bitterly cold, and the view was unremittingly monochrome: the trees stood out like black silhouettes against the white snow and the sky was grey and heavy, barely distinguishable from the dark, glacial grey of the loch.

Between them, the children had put together a very creditable plan of the castle in the innocent belief that it would be useful to Amanda's 'secret project' but she was becoming increasingly doubtful about the whole idea. It was all very well for Norris to talk about the appeal of remoteness and exclusivity, but Dundinnie was so far away from any town that it was ridiculous, and you didn't need to be an architect to work out that it would cost a fortune to convert the castle into the kind of place he had in mind.

And then there was the weather. It hadn't stopped snowing since Iain had driven them back from the village three days ago. Amanda didn't mind it when it was cold and clear, but the unrelenting snow made it impossible to do anything but huddle round the fire, and the children were all heartily bored. They would have died rather than admit it, but she was sure that they would much rather have been at school with their friends.

There were still eight days to go until Christmas—too long to start getting excited about stockings and decorations. She would have suggested taking them to Edinburgh for a couple of days, just to break the monotony, but Blair would just tell her that he was paying her good money to entertain them, or something equally disagreeable.

After he had slammed back into his study, Amanda had

spent the day in high dudgeon. It hadn't been that she was particularly anxious to see Iain again, but Blair had had no right to treat her as if she were some kind of slave!

With the help of Maggie's recipe books, supper that night had been a marked improvement on her first effort, but he hadn't even noticed. Nor had he seemed to realise that Amanda had been at her most dignified. Far from being quelled by her icy composure, he had simply announced that he was going to carry on working and had shut himself in his study, thus depriving Amanda of the chance to show him how little the previous night's kiss had affected her.

She'd spent the evening staring at the same page of a book and telling herself that she was heartily glad that she didn't have to spend any more time with him than necessary, but whenever she'd tried to concentrate on the printed words in front of her the memory of the kiss had shimmered between her and the page, prickling over her skin and booming through her veins. Blair was arrogant, insufferable, a bully, so why couldn't she forget the gasping excitement of his lips on hers?

It had been the same for the last three days. Blair had emerged for meals, but otherwise Amanda and the children had been left to their own devices. They were on the best of terms by now, largely because Amanda let them watch television whenever they wanted. They were all slumped in front of it now. Having cleared up after lunch, Amanda was morosely sipping a cup of coffee and deciding that this month was turning out to be a complete waste of time. What was the point of her spending a month looking at snow? Norris would probably have forgotten about her existence by the time she got back to London, and reminding him of it just to point out the unsuitability of his pet project was hardly likely to further her prospects of promotion.

It wouldn't be so bad if Blair hadn't turned out to be so unpleasant. He so rarely came out of his study that he probably wouldn't notice whether she was there or not. He had obviously never heard that Christmas was supposed to be the season of goodwill. She had a good mind to leave him to look after his nephews and niece himself. At least there would be something to *do* in London. If it hadn't been for Sue and the need to maintain her reputation with the agency, she'd go tomorrow and let Blair McAllister stew!

'I wish Uncle Blair had a video,' sighed Simon as the credits rolled up after *Neighbours*.

'I wish Uncle Blair had a different personality,' said Amanda sourly.

'Unfortunately for you both, Uncle Blair has no intention of acquiring either,' said a dry voice from behind them, and Amanda swung round so guiltily that she slopped coffee all the way down her jumper. 'Look at you all!' Blair went on as she dabbed crossly at the stain. 'What are you doing sitting around the television in the middle of the day?' He strode over and switched it off to a chorus of protests. 'You're all coming out with me…and that includes you, Amanda,' he said before she could excuse herself.

Amanda looked at him, affronted. She might have been complaining to herself about his unsociable habits, but that didn't mean she wanted to be dragged outside into the cold. 'I thought you were working?' she grumbled.

'I need a break,' he said. 'And you all need some fresh air and exercise. You haven't been outside the castle all week.'

'Yes, we have,' protested Amanda. 'And we got extremely wet and extremely cold, which is what we'll get again if we go out with you now.'

'Nonsense,' said Blair briskly. 'You just need the right clothes on. Go and put on extra jumpers and a waterproof and we'll take the toboggans. We may as well make the most of the snow.'

The children were thrilled with the four rather rusty sledges he produced from one of the stables. Amanda, bullied into an old anorak and gumboots, trudged along behind them as they dragged the toboggans out to where a steep hillside swept down into an open field. Normally it was covered with yellow, tussocky grass but the snow had smoothed everything into one long, clean sweep of white, and in spite of her determination to resent Blair's high-handed ways Amanda felt her spirits rise. The cold stung her cheeks and set her teeth on edge when she breathed in, but at least it had stopped snowing. Blair had probably arranged that too.

Stumbling a little over the uneven ground, she followed the others as they galloped up the hill. 'This is where we used to race when we were children,' said Blair, surveying the scene with a reminiscent air. 'You can get up quite a speed down here. Come on; we'll have our own race and see if these things still go as fast as they used to.'

The boys were raring to go, but Emily lost her nerve at the last minute and said that she would rather go with Blair. That left a sledge for Amanda. She lined it up with the others and sat down astride it as they waited for Blair to give the signal, and the next minute they were off, shooting down through the snow and bumping wildly over the rough patches to lurch to a halt out in the field, all laughing and whooping with exhilaration.

Amanda had never seen Blair look so relaxed. He held Emily securely against him, shielding her from the worst of the bumps and she couldn't help thinking how wonderful it would feel to skim over the snow, knowing that his arms were about you and you were utterly safe. His smile kept catching at the edge of her vision and an unsettling, exhilarating warmth uncurled somewhere deep inside her and seeped outwards until she had forgotten all about being cold.

They dragged the toboggans back to the top of the hill and flew down again, the boys each managing a spectacular crash at the bottom that only seemed to increase their enthusiasm. Up at the top for the third time, Emily decided at the last minute that she wanted to go by herself.

'You take Amanda's sledge,' said Blair. 'It's lighter than this one. Amanda can come with me.'

Having watched Emily with something like envy, Amanda now found herself strangely reluctant to take her place. The sledge seemed tiny as Blair shifted himself back and patted the seat in front of him, apparently quite unselfconscious. She could hardly refuse to go with him, though, so she avoided his eyes and settled herself down, trying not to lean against him but burningly aware of the strength and warmth of his body and of his arms reaching round her for the rope to steer the toboggan.

Relax, she told herself sternly as they waited, poised at the top of the hill, to see that Emily made it safely down to the bottom. As she jumped up, shrieking with delight, Blair pulled Amanda back hard against him and dug his boots into the snow to send them hurtling down the hill in their turn.

Their combined weight made the toboggan go much faster but to Amanda the descent seemed to last for ever. She was intensely conscious of Blair, of the sound of the sledge shushing through the snow, of the tiny snowflakes stinging her cheeks, and she was suddenly, wildly, happy, whooping with sheer joy as they careered past Simon and came at last to a lurching halt. For an instant Blair's arms tightened around her to steady her, and then the magical trip was over and he was reaching down to pull her to her feet.

There was an odd, unreadable expression in his eyes and Amanda's smile faltered. It was impossible to tell what he was thinking. Was he irritated by her yells, or had he too felt that surge of euphoria? Realising that she was still holding onto his gloved hand, she pulled her own hastily away and tried to cover her sudden awkwardness by turning to watch the children, who were shrieking with excitement as they hurtled down the hill again. They were hardly recognisable as the children who had sat slumped in front of the television less than an hour ago. Their eyes were bright and their faces pink and glowing.

'You were right about coming out,' she said to Blair. 'They're loving it.' She hesitated, brushing the clogged snow off the bottom of her trousers. 'I'm sorry I was so grumpy about the whole idea.'

'I'm the one who should apologise,' said Blair. 'I've been so busy trying to finish my manuscript that I haven't paid the children enough attention. I should be spending more time with them.'

Dragging the sledge out of the way, he sat down on it sideways, shifting to make room for Amanda, and for a few minutes they watched the children in a silence that was for once not uncomfortable. 'It must bring back memories for you, seeing the children here,' she said after a while.

'Yes, it does,' said Blair. 'There were three of us too.'

'Three?' Amanda looked at him in surprise. 'I got the impression that Belinda was your only sister.'

'She is. Malcolm was our cousin.' Blair didn't take his eyes off Nicholas's small figure as he toiled up the hill with his sledge. 'He was killed in a car accident eleven years ago.'

Amanda remembered now Maggie saying something about a Malcolm. 'I'm sorry,' she said inadequately. 'Were you very close?'

Blair didn't answer her question directly. 'I used to hero-worship him when I was younger,' he said. 'Everybody loved Malcolm. For most of his life it seemed as if he had everything. He was very intelligent, a natural sportsman, and he had that sort of reckless charm that most people find impossible to resist. Malcolm never did anything by halves. If he was happy, he was happier than anyone else had ever been before; and, in the same way, he was never just a bit down, he was in the depths of despair.'

He paused as if something had just occurred to him, and glanced down at Amanda sitting next to him on the sledge with a frown that was almost puzzled. 'He was a bit like you that way,' he said slowly. 'There was nothing moderate about Malcolm either, and he had the same ability to light up a room just by walking into it.'

He sounded so taken aback by the thought that Amanda felt her cheeks grow hot. She wasn't at all sure how to react. 'He sounds great,' she said awkwardly in the end.

'Yes…yes, he was.' Blair seemed to have forgotten her again. 'I was just twelve when I came to live at Dundinnie after my parents were killed. Bindie—that's what we used to call Belinda—was only eight. It was a black time for both of us, but Malcolm made life exciting again. He was four years older than I was. A lot of sixteen-year-old boys wouldn't have been bothered with kids, but he let us tag along with whatever he was doing. He taught us how to sail and how to find our way around the hills, and when it snowed he brought us here and made everything fun.

'I thought we were close.' He answered Amanda's question at last. 'We *were* close until—' He stopped then, obviously thinking better of what he had been about to say. He had worn a far-away expression as he'd remembered his cousin, but all at once he seemed to recall where he was, and who was sitting next to him. 'Until he was killed,' he finished eventually.

'I'm sorry,' said Amanda again, unable to think of anything else to say. She watched Nicholas and Simon rough-and-tumbling in the snow, oblivious to the fact that they were soaking wet, and thought about Blair as a little boy, hardly older than Simon, whose world had been turned upside down, and about Malcolm who had offered him comfort when he'd most needed it.

'I didn't realise,' she went on after a while. 'You seem so much part of Dundinnie that I assumed you'd always been here.'

'No.' Blair's eyes rested on the irregular lines of the castle down by the loch. 'No, Dundinnie was always Malcolm's.'

'Is that why you travel so much? Because you feel Dundinnie isn't really your home?'

She suspected that the glib psychology had irritated him, and it seemed at first as if he wasn't going to answer. The blue-grey gaze flickered to her face and then back to the castle. 'Maybe,' he said at last, as if unwilling to admit even that much.

Amanda drew a deep breath. 'Have you ever thought about selling it?'

'Sell Dundinnie?' Blair looked at her, incredulous at the very idea.

'Why not? You spend more time overseas than you do here and it must cost a fortune to keep up. If you don't feel that you really belong here—'

'I didn't say that,' he said sharply. 'There's no way I'd ever sell Dundinnie, no matter how much it cost me to keep it going. Even if I didn't want to live here myself, I would have to keep it in trust for Simon. If I don't have a son of my own, then he'll inherit Dundinnie eventually.'

Amanda found that she didn't want to think about Blair with a son, and concentrated on Simon instead. 'Do you think he would want to live up here?' she asked doubtfully, and Blair nodded his head over to where Simon was standing on his sledge and shouting for what seemed the sheer pleasure of it.

'He might if he spends more time discovering what makes Dundinnie special and less in front of the television,' he said. 'And a lot of that is up to me, I know.'

She had asked, and Blair had said that he wouldn't sell. Amanda felt obscurely relieved. If he had indicated that he would be interested in selling, she might have had to confess what she was doing and start negotiating, but, as it was, she could report to Norris with a clear conscience. He would have to look elsewhere for his health centre. Dundinnie wasn't for sale.

CHAPTER SIX

AMANDA was very quiet as they made their way back to Dundinnie through the snow. She had been so busy resenting Blair for the way he made her feel that it hadn't occurred to her that he would have feelings of his own. She had glimpsed another side of him today: the Blair who had been a small boy, confused and miserable after the death of his parents and clinging to the kindness of his older cousin; the Blair who had once found Dundinnie as cold and intimidating as she did; the Blair who had grieved for Malcolm and perhaps still felt guilty about taking his place.

The children ran ahead, in manic high spirits, and their laughter was so infectious that Amanda couldn't help smiling. It was already starting to get dark and the snow was drifting slowly down again in huge, soft flakes that clung to her lashes. 'It's just like walking through a Christmas card, isn't it?' she said to Blair, and, carried away by a rush of Christmas feeling, she lifted her voice and began to sing a tuneless but energetic rendition of 'A Partridge in a Pear Tree'.

Hearing her voice, the children stopped and waited for them to catch up, ready to join in with a chorus of 'five go-old rings'. After that they sang 'Good King Wenceslas' and 'White Christmas' twice, and they were still singing about sleigh-bells ringing as they stamped the snow off their boots at the back door. Amanda felt like a child again. It had been years since she had had that sense of Christmas as a time of wonder and joy and stomach-churning excitement.

'Can we buy a tree?' she asked Blair eagerly.

'Certainly not,' he said, and then grinned at her disappointed expression. 'I'm not paying for a tree when there are thousands

94

of fir trees growing on the estate. I'll get Murdoch to pick us out a nice one.'

'What about decorations?' she said, trying to tell herself that it was all the singing that had made her breathless and absolutely nothing to do with his smile.

'That I'm not sure about.' Blair opened the door and the children tumbled inside like puppies. 'There certainly used to be some, but it's been so long since anyone had Christmas here that I've no idea where they would be. Still, I can't imagine that they would have been thrown away. We can have a look for them tomorrow, if you like.'

Emily was tugging at his sleeve. 'Can't we look for them now?'

'Tomorrow,' said Blair.

'Oh, please, please, please…'

'Tomorrow,' he said again firmly, and looked up to see Amanda laughing at the pleading look on Emily's face, which seemed to suggest that the world would end if she couldn't look for the decorations that very instant.

Amanda's face was alight with amusement. A few snow-flakes still clung to her hair and she seemed to glow with vitality. Blair had been smiling too, but his grin faded as he looked at Amanda and the slate-coloured eyes blazed with an expression that made Amanda's own smile falter. 'Is something the matter?' she asked uncertainly.

'No.' He was curt to the point of rudeness as he turned abruptly away. He strode off down the passage only to stop at the top of the stairs to the kitchen and turn back, scowling. 'You can have an evening off whenever you want,' he said brusquely, as if she had spent the afternoon pestering him about it. 'Use the phone in my study to ring your doctor if you want.'

Amanda stared after him as he stomped off down the stairs, shouting to the children to change their wet clothes. She felt utterly confused. What was he so cross about? If he didn't want her to take an evening off, all he had to do was say so. Hanging up her jacket with a sigh, she reflected that it had been much easier when Blair had been grumpy all the time. At least she'd known where she was with him then. Now he was either smiling at her and making her like him against her will or glowering at her as if he hated her. It was very unsettling.

An evening spent in Iain Ferguson's good-humoured company would make a nice change, Amanda told herself, but was guiltily aware that she felt less than enthusiastic at the prospect. Still, she might as well take advantage of an evening off cooking.

Iain was delighted when Amanda rang him, and arranged to pick her up at seven o'clock the following evening, snow permitting. 'You didn't waste much time, did you?' said Blair sardonically when she went downstairs to tell him.

'You said it would be all right,' Amanda reminded him stiffly.

He was cutting a slice of bread with a sort of ferocious energy. 'I didn't realise you were that desperate to get away!'

'If it's not convenient, I'll ring Iain and arrange another day—' she began, but he interrupted her with an irritable wave of the knife.

'No, no, you go if you're so keen to see him!'

Amanda gave up, in as bad a mood as he by now. If Blair wanted to be difficult, let him! She made the tea instead, thumping the teapot down by the kettle and crashing the plates together. Blair ignored her until, provoked beyond endurance by the way she was slamming knives down onto the table, he looked up with an exclamation of exasperation. Amanda met his gaze defiantly, her own bright with temper, and for a tense moment they glared at each other across the kitchen.

And then, quite suddenly, they both realised how childishly they were behaving, and they began to laugh at the absurdity of it all. 'I'm sorry,' Blair apologised when they had recovered. 'Tomorrow night's fine. I don't mind you going out at all.'

Somehow it wasn't quite what Amanda had wanted to hear.

Exhausted by the fresh air and exercise, the children put up no resistance to going to bed that evening. When she had said goodnight to them all, Amanda collapsed into an armchair in the sitting room and kicked off her shoes. She felt physically weary, but the exhilarated relief of the moment when Blair had thrown back his head and laughed with her was still buzzing beneath her skin.

He was sitting opposite her now, feet, like hers, stretched out towards the fire, turning a glass of whisky absently between his hands. The intangible bond that they had discovered as they'd burst into laughter together had vanished, and he was once more withdrawn and preoccupied by his own thoughts. The silence was not uncompanionable, though, and Amanda was content to sit curled up in the shabby chair and watch him from under her lashes.

Outside, it was dark and very cold, but the sitting room was warm and safe and felt like home. Amanda felt as if the two of them were quite alone, isolated from the rest of the world, marooned together in the semicircle of firelight while time— real time—slowed and stopped.

It was such a strange, magical feeling that when Blair leant forward to add a log to the fire and stir it with his toe she caught her breath. The flames guttered, spluttered, then burned up once more, throwing flickering shadows over his face and dissolving the remoteness of his expression. There was something elusive about him, Amanda thought. Just when she thought she knew what he was like, he would turn his head or smile or simply lean into the firelight, as now, and her image of him would shift and splinter, rearranging itself into a new and unfamiliar pattern.

Would the pattern ever fix itself in her mind? Would she ever know what he was really like?

No, she wouldn't be here long enough to find that out. How could a month be long enough to discover what made anyone tick, let alone a complex man like Blair McAllister? Amanda was gripped by a sudden sadness to realise that Blair would never be utterly familiar to her. She would never know every crease around his eyes, every turn of his head. His taste and his smell and the texture of his skin would never be as familiar to her as her own.

The longing to see him glance up and smile and reassure her was so strong that Amanda was afraid that she was going to shout it out loud and she had to press her lips tight together. Why should Blair care how well she knew him? She was a stranger, no more than a temporary disturbance to his routine.

An impostor.

All at once the enormity of her behaviour hit her with the force of a blow. She had been so arrogant, so determined to impress Norris Jeffries that she hadn't given a thought to how Blair might feel at taking a perfect stranger into his home under false pretences, or paying for someone utterly unqualified to look after his sister's children.

Amanda squirmed in her chair. Taking Sue's place had seemed such a good idea at the time. She had brushed aside every objection to ensure that she got her own way, without thinking how it might affect anyone else. She was selfish and thoughtless and irresponsible, and if Blair knew the truth he would pack her onto the first train home. That was all she deserved.

Consumed with guilt, Amanda opened her mouth to confess everything and beg his forgiveness, only to shut it again. Sue's reputation would be ruined if the agency heard what she had done, and she would find it difficult to get another job without a reference. Amanda bit her lip. Sue hadn't wanted to let Amanda take her place and had only allowed herself to be persuaded against her better judgement. If she confessed now, she would be sacrificing Sue's career for her own peace of mind, Amanda realised bleakly. She had behaved irresponsibly enough as it was. Her first concern should be to protect her friend, not ease her conscience.

Protecting Sue meant deceiving Blair. Amanda stared miserably into the fire. It was hard now to remember how important her job with Norris Jeffries had seemed. Did she really want to spend her life in an office, rushing from crisis to crisis for no better cause than Norris's profits? And if that wasn't what she wanted, what *did* she want?

Amanda's mind flickered to Blair before she clamped resolutely down on a train of thought that threatened to become dangerous. There was no future for her here, and the sooner she accepted that the better. Belinda would come back from New Zealand and Blair would put her, Amanda, on the train back to London, no doubt with a sigh of relief. In the meantime, the least she could do to make up for her deception was to earn Sue's salary for her.

She would be the best nanny ever, Amanda vowed. She would cook and she would clean and take the children out instead of letting them watch television all day, and she would make sure that this Christmas was one for them to remember. As for Norris, well, she would just say that Dundinnie was quite unsuitable for development.

Decision made, Amanda began to feel a little better. She was still uncomfortable about deceiving Blair, though, and as she glanced across at him she wished passionately that she was there in her own right and not as an impostor. She wished that he would look up and smile at her.

She wished he would kiss her again.

The thought caught her unawares. She felt jarred, slightly sick, as if she had walked into a wall in the dark. Desperately, she tried to blank the idea out of her mind, but her eyes kept crawling across to Blair as if they had a will of their own. She stared at his fingers curled around his glass and imagined how they would feel curling around her hand, pulling her down onto his lap. Wrenching her gaze away made no difference. The next minute her eyes skittered back to his mouth and she found herself remembering how it had relaxed into a smile, remembering how warm and exciting it had been, imagining how it would be if his lips were drifting along her jaw towards hers right now...

Amanda felt as if she was dissolving inside, as if sensation was pooling into a deep, unsettling warmth that threatened to spill over at any moment. And Blair was just sitting there, calmly drinking his whisky as if she weren't even *there*!

The realisation made Amanda swing her legs abruptly to the floor. 'I'm tired,' she said, horrified at how tight and high her voice sounded. 'I think I'll go to bed.'

What was she expecting? That he would beg her not to go? That he would sweep her off her feet and lay her down on the hearth-rug in front of the fire?

'Goodnight,' he said, and went back to his whisky.

Amanda went down to breakfast the next day still fired with resolution to be the perfect nanny. Perfect nannies were calm and sensible and concentrated on the children; they didn't waste their time on ridiculous fantasies about their employer, and nor would she. Amanda had spent most of the night convincing herself that she hadn't really wanted Blair to kiss her. She had just been...tired. It was a pretty lame explanation, she knew, but it was the best she could come up with.

Mindful of her newly efficient character, she checked the fridge and the freezer after breakfast. 'We could do with some more bread and milk,' she said to Blair, who was finishing a cup of coffee. 'Will I be able to get some more at the village shop?'

'You should be able to.' He looked up. 'Do you want me to drive you down?'

Amanda glanced out of the window. The temperature had risen overnight and a pale, wintry sun was struggling to melt the icicles hanging from the gutter. 'It's a nice day,' she said. 'I think I'll walk.'

Blair eyed her humorously. 'You've changed,' he commented, and Amanda paused in the middle of scribbling herself a list.

'Yes,' she said slowly. 'I'm beginning to think I have.'

The children were lurking, waiting to pounce on Blair and make him fulfil his promise of looking for the decorations, so Amanda left them to it and set off at a brisk pace. It was wonderful to see the sun again and her spirits rose with every step. Had she and Emily really made such a fuss about trailing along this same road only a few days ago? Swinging along in the cold, clear air, Amanda found that it took her no time at all, and by the time she got back to Dundinnie her cheeks were glowing with the exercise.

She heard the tell-tale ping of the phone being put down as she opened the door, and the next minute Blair appeared at his study door. 'That was your agency,' he began, and then stopped as he saw Amanda. Her sherry-coloured eyes were bright and sparkling, and she looked both young and astonishingly vivid against the austere stone walls of the great hall.

'My agency?' she said stupidly, lowering the carrier bags to the floor.

Blair seemed to recollect himself. 'Yes, they were calling from London. I couldn't think who they were talking about at first when they asked to speak to Susan Haywood!'

Amanda's heart gave a huge lurch. 'What did they want?'

'Just to find out how you were getting on and to check that everything was OK. They said that you usually rang after the first few days.'

'Oh, yes,' said Amanda weakly. 'I forgot.'

'It didn't seem to matter,' said Blair, leaning against the doorjamb. 'I told them that you were fine, and they seemed

quite happy. They wanted to know how things were going,
and whether I was pleased with you or not.'

'What did you say?' she nerved herself to ask.

'Well, I had to point out that I hadn't expected someone
quite so argumentative, of course, and then there was your
bizarre fantasy life and utter lack of discipline, and the grump-
iness in the mornings…' Blair shook his head sadly, then saw
Amanda's doubtful expression and relented with a smile. 'Actually, I said you were doing a fantastic job. The kids think
you're great.'

And you? Amanda wanted to ask. She could feel the
warmth of his smile uncurling within her, spilling along her
veins to seep over her skin, but consciousness of her own
duplicity made her awkward. 'You didn't mention my cooking, then?' she said huskily.

'Your cooking's not so bad,' said Blair. 'It's certainly improved out of all recognition since you arrived. In fact,' he
went on slowly, 'everything about you has improved since you
arrived.'

Amanda felt as if her heart had slowed right down, making
it a struggle to breathe. She couldn't think of anything to say,
could only look back at him and feel the warmth deepening
and spreading. For a long moment they just looked at each
other, and then Blair turned back to his study. 'Oh, by the
way, your doctor friend rang as well,' he added in a gruff
voice. 'The gritters have been out, so there won't be any problem about the roads. He's going to pick you up at seven.'

'Oh.' Amanda felt stupidly deflated. He obviously couldn't
care whether she went out with Iain or not. It was very lucky
that she had been out when the agency rang, as they would
certainly have recognised that it wasn't Sue on the other end
of the phone. A terrible thought struck her. What if Norris
were to do the same? Proud of her own initiative, she had told
him that she had arranged to spend several weeks in
Dundinnie, but she hadn't said anything about Sue. She

wouldn't put it past him to ring and find out how much progress she had made, and if Blair answered the phone he would want to know exactly who Amanda was.

Amanda's blood ran cold at the prospect of the ensuing confrontation. Wouldn't it be better to ring Norris herself to forestall any move on his part? 'Um…Blair?' she said hurriedly as he made to close the door. 'Do you think I could make a quick phone call?'

'Of course.' He held open the door. 'Come in.'

The last thing she wanted was for Blair to overhear her conversation with Norris! 'Er…it's rather private,' she said desperately as she went in, and his face shuttered.

'Ringing Hugh or another of that string of boyfriends?' he sneered. 'Don't worry, I was going to leave you alone while I went to find the children. Even I am not crass enough to hang around and eavesdrop on your private conversations, and I doubt if my stomach could stand it anyway!'

'No, you don't underst—' Amanda began, but he had gone, shutting the door behind him with something very close to a slam, and she was left staring at the place where he had been with a mixture of confusion, guilt and anger that he could be so blind. Surely he didn't think that she was still in love with Hugh? Amanda was astonished that Blair should even remember him. She had forgotten how she had apparently poured out her entire romantic history to Blair under the influence of his whisky. Was it really only a week ago? Already it seemed like part of another life, and Hugh a figure from a dream.

Sighing, she went over to the phone and dialled Norris's office number. 'Ah, Amanda, I was wondering when I was going to hear from you,' he said. 'How's it going?'

'Well, I've drawn up a plan,' she began, crossing her fingers as she thought about the pictures that the children had laboriously drawn for her. 'But I'm not sure it would be such a good investment,' she went on cautiously, hoping to dissuade him from the whole idea of transforming Dundinnie into a health centre—an idea which seemed more grotesque every time she thought about it now. 'The castle's not in very good condition, you know. It would need a huge amount of work doing to it.'

'Good,' was all Norris said. 'That'll bring the price down. Have you approached McAllister with an offer yet?'

'Not exactly.'

'What do you mean, "not exactly"?' he asked sharply. 'Either you have or you haven't. There's a lot riding on this project, Amanda. I've got everything else arranged, but I can't keep the financial boys hanging around for a decision much longer. We're all waiting for the go-ahead from you.'

Amanda's heart sank at his tone. Why hadn't she realised how ruthless he sounded before? 'He's told me that he would never consider selling Dundinnie, no matter what financial problems he had.'

Norris leapt on her words. 'So he has got financial problems?'

'Yes…no…not immediately.' Amanda was beginning to feel hunted. 'He's just finishing a book.'

'A book?' sneered Norris. 'A book won't pay for the upkeep of a place like Dundinnie! No, it sounds as if he's just been using the same fine words he used with me, but I don't think they mean much.'

'He isn't a man who says something he doesn't mean,' she snapped before she could help herself, and as soon as the words were out of her mouth she realised that she had made a mistake. There was an ominous pause at the other end of the phone.

'I'm disappointed in you, Amanda,' said Norris at last. 'I gave you the responsibility for this project because I thought you had a great future with my company, but you're not going to go very far if you're going to let yourself be put off just because of what a man says! No, you'd better come back and I'll find some way of tackling McAllister again myself.'

'No!' said Amanda in panic. Leave Dundinnie? Leave Blair and the children and spend Christmas in London? It was unthinkable! 'No. I mean, the thing is, Norris, I've got quite close to Blair over the last few days and I think if I stayed a bit longer I might be in a better position to persuade him.' Anything to put Norris off!

'That sound's more like it.' Norris laughed in a meaningful way. 'I knew you were the kind of girl who wasn't afraid to use whatever it took to get what she wanted,' he congratulated himself. 'There's nothing quite like a little old-fashioned seduction, is there? Those strong, silent types are always the most susceptible too. That's why I picked you. You're an attractive girl,' he went on with a joviality that grated down Amanda's spine. 'I knew Blair McAllister would be bound to notice.'

Her fingers clenched around the receiver. So much for Norris recognising her abilities! What a fool she had been, claiming him as her mentor when he viewed her as no more than a useful body to be bartered in exchange for a good deal. She felt sick, soiled, smirched by his sordid insinuations, but at least she had stopped him contacting Blair himself. When her time was up, she would go back to London and tell him what he could do with his job, but for now the important thing was to make sure that nothing spoiled Christmas. If that meant lying to Norris, then so be it.

'Let's just say I'm working on him,' she said, allowing her voice to drop suggestively. 'We're spending Christmas together, so it would be best if you didn't ring me.'

'What if something comes up this end?'

Amanda hesitated. 'Blair doesn't know that I'm working for you,' she confessed at last. 'If you have to ring, do you think you could pretend you were just a friend?'

'Covering your tracks?' guffawed Norris. 'Wise girl! OK, I won't ring you unless absolutely necessary, and you concen-

trate on making yourself irresistible to Blair McAllister. I'll
expect to hear from you at the end of December.'

Amanda was shaking when she put down the phone. Why
had she ever become involved with someone as sleazy as
Norris? She should never have come up here and involved
Blair in her pathetic ambitions. But if she had never come, a
small voice whispered, she would never have met him. She
wouldn't have learnt to like the children, and she wouldn't
have been looking forward to Christmas with nearly so much
anticipation.

The thought made Amanda feel better. She was a perennial
optimist, with an enviable ability to put aside anything she
would rather not think about in the belief that, left alone,
things generally worked out for the best. Now she decided to
get on with Christmas and worry about Norris afterwards.

She found the children in the sitting room, rummaging
through a huge box of dusty decorations. There was no sign
of Blair.

'Look what we've found!' cried Emily, brandishing a length
of rather thin-looking tinsel. 'Uncle Blair says we're to sort
through it and we can get some more if there isn't enough.'

'He's ordered a tree, too,' Nicholas piped up. 'It's coming
tomorrow.' Blair was obviously the hero of the hour.

'That's great,' said Amanda, trying not to wonder how she
could persuade Blair that she hadn't been ringing a boyfriend
without admitting the truth. She knelt down by the box. 'Well,
let's see what we've got here...'

They spent all afternoon sorting through the box, blowing
the dust off shiny baubles and straightening angels' wings and
singing 'White Christmas' again and again. Some of the decorations were set aside for the arrival of the tree the next day,
but everything else likely was pinned up or draped around the
room. The end result lacked style, perhaps, but not enthusiasm,
and as they brushed the dust from their hands they were well
pleased with their endeavours.

'It looks very…Christmassy,' said Amanda tactfully, kneeling to put all the broken bits and pieces back in the box.

They had drawn the curtains as it had grown dark and the fire was leaping and crackling. She wished guiltily that she didn't have to go out with Iain when she would much rather stay in this cosy room with Blair, even if he still hadn't come down off his high horse. He had been very cool at teatime. Perhaps it was just as well that she was going out, she decided with a sigh as she climbed stiffly to her feet.

Aware that she hadn't given a thought to Iain until now, Amanda salved her conscience by dressing with particular care that evening. She put on a pair of narrow trousers with a flame-coloured silk top, and brushed her hair until it shone and swung around her jaw.

When she went downstairs, she found the children sitting around the table eating a shepherd's pie that she had made earlier. Her cooking was still something less than accomplished, but she had mastered some of the basics. She and Blair usually ate with the children rather than cook two separate meals, but tonight he had obviously decided to make something for himself later. He was sitting at the table, going through a typescript while listening with half an ear to the children arguing about something.

Watching them from the doorway, Amanda was surprised by a rush of tenderness for them all, and for a wistful moment wished that she could sit down at the old, scrubbed table and eat shepherd's pie instead of being taken out to an expensive dinner. The realisation of just how much she had changed made her smile ruefully. She had come a long way since she had arrived in Scotland!

Blair looked up to see her still smiling. She looked warm and slender and vibrant as she stood there, the light gleaming on the nut-brown hair, the sherry-coloured eyes wide and bright. His hand froze in the middle of striking out a word.

'Why are you all dressed up?' demanded Nicholas, who had also caught sight of her.

'She's going out with Iain,' Emily informed him importantly. She had conceived a slavish adoration of Iain since he had saved her the walk back from the village and was far more excited about Amanda's night out with him than Amanda was. 'She looks beautiful, doesn't she?' she added with an envious sigh, resting her chin on her hand.

The boys made predictable gagging motions and Amanda grinned. 'Thank you, Emily,' she said, gently tugging a blonde pigtail.

Emily was put out that no one seemed to share her opinion. 'Don't you think so, Uncle Blair?' she insisted, and Amanda's eyes met his reluctantly over her small head.

His expression was quite unreadable and Amanda realised that she was holding her breath. *Did* he think she was beautiful? There were no clues in the opaque blue-grey gaze.

'Yes, she looks beautiful,' said Blair at last, but it was patently obvious that he said it only to indulge Emily. Amanda wanted to hit him.

The bell at the front door clanged at that moment, and Blair's voice hardened as he glanced back at Amanda. 'I just hope he's worth all the effort.'

She set her teeth at the implication that she had spent hours getting ready. 'I'm sure he will be,' she said grittily.

He *was*, she reassured herself as she sat with Iain in the echoing dining room of a local hotel. In spite of the puritanical surroundings, Iain lived up to her first impressions of him as warm, funny and good company. He was a nice, straightforward man, unlike *some* men she could mention. It wasn't Iain's fault that he didn't make her spine clench or her heart turn handsprings whenever he smiled.

And that was precisely why she enjoyed the evening so much, Amanda decided later. There was none of the simmering tension that made every encounter with Blair so unsettling,

and she could relax and enjoy Iain's undemanding company.
Still bruised from his divorce, Iain was as glad as she was
simply to sit and talk, and by the end of the evening Amanda
had the comfortable feeling that they were already friends.

It was just before midnight when he drove her back to
Dundinnie, parking the car a little way up the drive so as not
to disturb anyone and gallantly insisting on walking Amanda
to the door. 'Thank you for a lovely evening, Iain,' she said,
smiling. 'I've really enjoyed it.'

'We'll do it again some time, shall we?'

'I'd like that,' she said, and reached up quite naturally to
kiss his cheek.

'I thought I heard a car.' Blair's voice cut across her goodnight, as cold and cutting as the wind that always seemed to
be blowing off the sea, and she jerked round to see him tow-
ering in the open doorway.

She had little choice but to introduce the two men. Iain was
unselfconsciously delighted to meet someone whose work he
admired so much, but his enthusiasm could hardly have been
more in contrast with Blair's curt replies. Amanda was furious
with Blair for being so rude. In the face of his obvious lack
of encouragement, she could hardly invite Iain in for a coffee,
and it was equally obvious that he had no intention of leaving
them alone. She had to content herself with thanking Iain again
under Blair's blistering gaze.

Quite unfazed by Blair's hostility, Iain grinned, pleasantly
wished them both goodnight and walked back to his car. As
soon as he was out of earshot, Amanda turned on Blair.

'Did you have to be so rude to him?'

'What's the matter? Afraid he won't ask you out again?'

'I wouldn't blame him if he didn't!' Amanda stalked into
the hall, only just resisting the urge to slam the door in Blair's
face. 'No one in their right mind would run the risk of meeting
you again if they'd been treated the way you just treated Iain,
and I don't want to go out if it means being greeted by a

reception committee when I get back! You're worse than my father used to be!'

'You're just cross because I interrupted your fond farewell,' Blair jeered, following her inside. 'Or wasn't it going to be farewell? Were you hoping that I'd be in bed so that you could sneak him up to your room and add another scalp to your already crowded collection?'

Amanda's golden eyes flashed. 'Don't be ridiculous!' she snapped. 'I thought I was supposed to be the one with the vivid imagination?'

'It didn't take much imagination to see the inviting way you were kissing him!'

Drawing a deep breath, Amanda counted to ten. 'I was saying goodnight,' she said between her teeth.

'Do you always say goodnight with a kiss?' asked Blair savagely, and she rolled her eyes with an exaggerated sigh.

'Anyone would think you'd interrupted an orgy! I'd kiss anyone goodnight after we'd spent an evening together. It doesn't mean anything.'

'Now that I *can* believe!' he said.

'Good!' said Amanda. 'Now, if you'll excuse me…'

She turned towards the stairs only to find herself brought up short as Blair's hand closed around her wrist. 'Where are you going?'

'To bed,' she said, still too angry to be cautious. She tried to tug her arm free, but he only tightened his grip as he drew her towards him.

'Aren't you going to say goodnight?'

Even then she didn't make the connection. Her face was stormy as she glared up at him. She was tempted to refuse but he held her pinioned now and she was no match for his strength. 'Oh, very well…*goodnight*,' she said tightly.

Blair tutted. 'That's not how you said goodnight to Iain Ferguson, is it?'

He was daring her to kiss him. The fire faded from

Amanda's face as the realisation sank in, and her heart seemed to slow until every beat was an enormous effort. She stared uncertainly at him.

'Well?' he said sarcastically as she hesitated. 'I thought you'd kiss anyone goodnight? I thought it didn't mean anything?'

How could she explain that it was different with him? Amanda moistened her lips surreptitiously. 'I-it doesn't, but…'

'But what?' Blair loosed her wrists to grip her waist and pull her inexorably against him. 'What's one more kiss to a girl like you, Amanda?'

The unfair gibe helped her pull herself together. Stiffening angrily, she sucked in her breath. He needn't think the idea of kissing him worried *her*! She lifted herself jerkily up onto her toes and touched her lips to his cheek in a gesture that was meant to be as disdainful as it was brief.

Only it didn't quite work out like that. An electric awareness shuddered through her as soon as her lips grazed his skin. Blair must have felt it, but his hand was already at the nape of her neck, holding her still while his lips drifted along her cheek. 'That wasn't much of a goodnight,' he murmured against the corner of her mouth. 'I'm sure we can do better than that.'

His other arm gathered her close against him as he spoke. Determined to resist this time, Amanda screwed up her eyes and tensed, jamming her hands against his chest. She was so prepared for a punishing kiss that when it didn't come she opened her eyes again, puzzled.

Blair was looking down into her face. Amanda couldn't read his expression, but she had time to register that the tight, angry look had faded before he half smiled and touched his lips, very gently, to hers.

The tenderness of his kiss caught her unawares. She forgot that she could easily jerk her mouth away. She forgot that she was angry. She forgot everything but the astonishing sweet-

ness washing over her like sunlight. Insensibly, the hands
shoved against his chest relaxed, and the rigidity seeped out
of her body until she was melting into him, dizzy with delight.
She felt boneless, bewitched, blissfully adrift in intoxicating
pleasure, and when Blair lifted his head it was she who murmured an inarticulate protest. She didn't want him to stop. She
wanted this moment to go on and on for ever.

Blair's hold on her slackened as he drew an unsteady breath,
and then, with a savage exclamation, he jerked her back into
his arms. Amanda didn't even think to protest. She let him
crush her against him, glorying in the unyielding strength of
his body as the tenderness he had elicited so unexpectedly was
consumed by a fierce flame of desire that exploded in its turn
into a new urgency. Heedless of anything but the feel of him
and the taste of him and the wild, rocketing excitement,
Amanda wound her arms around Blair's neck and gave back
kiss for hungry kiss.

When his mouth left hers at last, she was breathless and
gasping, but as he began to drop scorching kisses along her
jaw she tipped back her head and smiled languidly, shivering
with pleasure at the tantalising progress of his lips, at the hard
insistence of his hand beneath her shirt. So abandoned was she
that she didn't at first realise that Blair was murmuring something in her ear between kisses.

'Hmm?' She didn't want to talk. She wanted him to sweep
her upstairs and peel off her clothes and lay her down on his
bed. And then...

'I said, That was much better, but I think we'd better say
goodnight while we still can, don't you?' Blair's voice was a
little ragged, but the irony was unmistakable.

It hit Amanda like a douse of cold water. Her arms fell from
his neck and she jerked backwards. She was trembling all over
and her eyes were huge and dark. 'You...you...'

'I what?'

'You shouldn't have done that,' she whispered.

Blair held up his hands in mock innocence. 'It was only a kiss, Amanda,' he said. 'And a kiss doesn't mean anything to you, does it?'

A wave of desolation hit her. How could he kiss her like that and then stand there and jeer? She opened her mouth to protest, but her throat was too tight to speak, and after one ghastly, frozen moment she turned with an abrupt movement and fled up the stairs to her room, caring only that Blair shouldn't see the tears coursing down her cheeks.

CHAPTER SEVEN

ANOTHER morning, another set of resolutions. Amanda looked into the mirror and grimaced at her reflection. She was tired of sleepless nights spent trying to push Blair's mouth and Blair's hands out of her memory, tired of convincing herself that his touch didn't really affect her at all, tired of having to brace herself anyway before she could face him in the morning. What was the point of her vowing to be cool, calm and collected when all it took was a look from him to reduce her to an incoherent, uncontrollable jumble of contradictory emotions?

Amanda didn't like feeling out of control. She wasn't used to it. *She* was the one who was supposed to be the free spirit, fascinating and exasperating boyfriends with her independence! It wasn't fair, the way Blair always managed to turn the tables on her and leave her feeling confused and humiliated and *cross*.

Fed up, Amanda went down to breakfast. The long, sleepless hours before dawn had finally succeeded in burying the memory of that devastating kiss beneath an avalanche of righteous anger that had put all the blame on Blair. He'd had no business kissing her like that. She was tired and gritty-eyed and out of temper, and it was all his fault.

Her mood was not improved by the fact that the children were all feeling chatty, or that Emily wanted to know about her evening out with Iain in exhaustive detail. Burningly aware of Blair's cool eyes on her, Amanda's answers were so curt that Simon was moved to ask her why she was so cross.

Amanda set her teeth. 'I am not cross!'

This was so patently untrue that the children didn't bother

to say anything. Blair took an unhurried sip of his coffee. 'Amanda's evening didn't end quite as she anticipated,' he explained with infuriating kindness, and Amanda clenched her fists.

Emily was looking worried. 'You're not angry with Iain, are you, Amanda?'

'No, not with *Iain*,' she said with a glare down the table that made it clear whom she *was* cross with, but, far from quailing, as anyone with any decency would have done, Blair merely lifted an eyebrow, the blandness of his expression a provocation in itself.

The children had resigned themselves to the fact that Amanda was not going to be much fun that morning and took the first opportunity to beat a tactical retreat. She hoped that Blair would follow their example, but he stayed to finish his coffee, quite unperturbed by the prickly silence. Determined not to be the one to break it—what did *she* have to be uncomfortable about?—she began clearing the table with much clattering of plates.

'I hate to point it out, but that's Spode you're taking out your bad temper on,' said Blair mildly at last.

Amanda's only answer was to slam the tops onto the jars of jam and honey and screw them down savagely. She could feel him watching her, but she refused to meet his eyes.

He sighed. 'All right,' he said. 'I'm sorry. I shouldn't have kissed you last night.'

'Is that supposed to make me feel better?' She crashed the washing-up bowl into the sink and aimed a jet of detergent under the hot water.

'What *would* make you feel better?'

'An assurance that it won't happen again, for a start!'

'Of course,' he said after a tiny pause. 'I can't say I didn't enjoy it, but I really didn't mean to kiss you. I was in a bad mood when you came back and I'm afraid I took it out on you. If it's any comfort, I took myself unawares quite as much as you.'

Amanda still couldn't look at him. She was concentrating fiercely on watching the bowl fill up with water. She had squirted in far too much washing-up liquid and now the bubbles were threatening to overwhelm the sink.

'Come on, Amanda,' Blair went on cajolingly. 'It was only a kiss!'

Only a kiss? 'I'm not used to being kissed like that!' she said, still huffy.

'Nor am I.' There was an odd note in his voice and all at once the kitchen was reverberating with the memory of the passion that had flared so unexpectedly between them last night.

Amanda kept her back turned and resolutely began washing up. 'Perhaps in future you could remember that I'm here to entertain the children, not you,' she said at last. That was it, just the right note of martyred dignity.

It didn't seem to impress Blair. 'I won't lay a finger on you again,' he said, hardly even bothering to keep the amusement from his voice. 'Unless specifically requested to do so, of course!'

'Don't hold your breath!' she snapped, slamming the frying-pan onto the draining-board.

She could feel his eyes boring into her back as she continued to wash up noisily, and kept her temper at boiling point by imagining his expression. He would be looking bored, perhaps exasperated, or, even worse, entertained by her hostility, but, knowing Blair, he certainly wouldn't be looking the way he *should* be looking, which was awkward or embarrassed. No, he would just be sitting there in that cool, quiet way of his, drinking his coffee and not caring in the least that she was cross and miserable!

When she heard the sound of Blair pushing back his chair and standing up, Amanda stiffened. That was it! Not content with humiliating her, he was just going to go away and leave her to her bad temper! Why didn't he do something to make her feel better, like putting his arms around her and letting her lean back against him and kissing her neck?

To her fury, Amanda felt tears sting her eyes. God, what was the *matter* with her? She was so busy blinking away the tears that she didn't at first realise that Blair hadn't left at all but had picked up a teatowel and was calmly drying the plates.

'Look, we can't fight all Christmas,' he said. 'It's not fair on the children. I really *am* sorry for kissing you, Amanda. I know I shouldn't have done.' He paused and glanced at her averted face. She didn't say anything, but she was listening. 'I know I haven't been easy to live with, either. I've had various things on my mind, and what with the deadline and the kids and then you… Well, anyway, I'm sorry,' he said again, evidently changing his mind about saying any more. 'We didn't get off on the right foot, did we?'

'No,' she muttered.

'Why don't we agree to start again?' said Blair, laying another plate onto the pile he had dried. 'I don't ask you to forgive me, but we could agree to forget about what's gone before and try to concentrate on making Christmas as enjoyable as possible for the children instead.'

Fat chance she had of forgetting his kiss, Amanda thought to herself, but what could she say? She couldn't sulk till she left.

'I'm prepared to try harder if you will,' he went on persuasively when she hesitated. 'But it does take two.'

Like a kiss. Amanda bit her lip. Blair could have pointed out that she had kissed him just as much as he had kissed her, she admitted honestly, but he had left her some shreds of pride to cling to after all.

'Well, what do you say?' he asked.

She drew a deep breath. 'All right,' she said, and looked at him at last. 'We'll start again.'

'Good,' he said, and smiled in what might have been relief.

Amanda thought the smile was unfair. She had wanted to keep a few shreds of dignity to soothe her pride, but all he had to do was smile and every last resistance crumbled, leaving her nothing to do but smile back.

As soon as they realised that they were just standing smiling at each other, both stopped and looked away. There was an awkward pause. Blair cleared his throat. 'Since the children are out of the way, I wanted to ask your advice,' he said with a sort of forced briskness after a moment. 'I need to buy them all a Christmas present. What do you think they'd like?'

'I...don't know,' said Amanda, still trying to steady her heart after that smile.

'I thought with your experience of children that you might have some good ideas.'

His words made her wince inwardly. She had let herself be so carried away with indignation at that kiss that she had forgotten just how much she was deceiving him.

'I've been thinking of what to give them myself,' she said. 'But I've always been an impulse buyer. I can never decide what to get until I see it, and then it just jumps out at me and I have to buy it even though it usually works out to be twice as much as I was intending to spend.'

'Yes, that's just how I would imagine you shopping,' said Blair, amused. He hesitated. 'Look, can you face another long drive? If I get Maggie to keep an eye on the children, we could go shopping tomorrow. We may as well make the most of the thaw as they say it's going to get colder again at the end of the week, and it might be as well to stock up on food too in case we can't get out again for a while.'

'That would be wonderful!' Amanda's face lit up. The village shop was fine for the basics, but she had been wondering where she was going to buy presents for the children. Already she had been away from London long enough to find the prospect of shopping exciting—at least, she told herself it was that and nothing to do with the idea of spending a day alone with Blair. Really, she was pathetic. Only minutes ago she had been furious with him, and now she could hardly remember why. It was lucky that she had been born in boring old England; she would have been hopeless at any kind of vendetta. 'I'll make a list,' she said happily.

She was still scribbling when the clanging of the bell announced the arrival of the Christmas tree. In fact, the men had brought two trees, one enormous one for the hall and a smaller one for the sitting room, along with great bunches of holly and mistletoe. Both trees were so tall that Amanda had to stand on a stepladder to fix the angels on top. She had been thrilled to discover holders for real candles in the box, and although the idea of all those naked flames seemed fraught with danger she couldn't resist clipping them on, seduced by the romantic image of them all gathered round the tree and lighting the candles on Christmas Eve.

'Candles', she scrawled on her list, and then added 'lights for tree' when they discovered that the fairy lights they had laboriously draped around the tree in the hall didn't work.

After lunch they left Blair working and went for a walk in the woods, where they gathered great armfuls of pine cones to pile into bowls. Emily wanted glittery paint added to the shopping list so that they could spray them all gold, but Amanda thought privately that she would contrive to forget it. She preferred the cones the way they were, filling the rooms with the clean, resinous smell of the woods.

'What are we going to do with all this mistletoe?' Simon kicked at it disparagingly.

Amanda looked at the mistletoe. She had been trying to avoid thinking about the mistletoe. What was it Emily had said when they had talked about it before? 'You can kiss Uncle Blair.' If she put up mistletoe now, it would look as if she wanted him to kiss her just as he had done last night, but if she *didn't* hang some somewhere it might be too obvious. She didn't want Blair to think she was making a big deal about kissing him...

'Why don't we hang a bunch under the light?' she suggested, hoping she sounded casual and not as if she had worked out that she was hardly likely to be hanging around right in the middle of the room looking as if she was waiting to be kissed. Anyway, the ceilings were so high in here that the chances were that Blair wouldn't even notice it.

Having reassured herself, Amanda tied a bunch of mistletoe together and dragged the stepladder back out once more. She clenched the string in her mouth while she teetered precariously right on top of the ladder and tried to work out how best to secure it.

Blair chose that moment to walk in. He took in Amanda's perilous position on top of the stepladder and roared at her to come down at once. 'Do you want to break your neck for the sake of a bunch of mistletoe?' he shouted, snatching the string out of her mouth as she wobbled back down the ladder almost in spite of herself. 'That *would* make for a jolly Christmas, wouldn't it?'

'You just can't bear the idea of having to go and pick up another nanny,' muttered Amanda, scarlet at having been caught in the very act. So much for sneaking the mistletoe up somewhere where Blair wouldn't notice it! It was absolutely typical of him to have come in then instead of two minutes later.

'It would certainly be extremely inconvenient,' said Blair coldly. 'Here, you hold the ladder and I'll tie this stuff up, since it means so much to you.'

Amanda was strongly tempted to push the ladder over, but she managed to content herself with pressing her lips together and waiting in simmering silence until, with characteristic competence, he had secured the mistletoe and climbed back down. 'You don't seem to have any idea about safety,' he harangued her, and Amanda was too mortified even to consider that he might actually have been worried when he came in and saw her swaying five feet above the ground. 'Surely it wouldn't have taken much common sense to have asked Simon to hold the ladder for you at the very least?'

'Oh, look, you're both standing under the mistletoe now,' squealed Emily, whose timing was almost as immaculate as her uncle's. 'Now you'll have to kiss!'

'Frankly, Emily, your uncle is the last person I'd be prepared to kiss right at this moment!' snapped Amanda, too cross to be embarrassed. 'Being lectured on common sense doesn't make me feel very romantic!'

To her fury, she saw amusement lighten Blair's black scowl. 'Oh, come on, don't be a spoilsport,' he said provocatively, and before she realised quite what he was doing he had slid a hand to the nape of her neck and was drawing her towards him. Very deliberately, he kissed the corner of her mouth.

His lips were cool and firm, and Amanda's heart did the kind of somersault that would have had the judges leaping to their feet with scores of ten at an Olympic gymnastic event. Her skin was tingling where he touched it and she had to struggle against the overwhelming urge to turn her face so that her mouth could meet his. An inch—that was all it would take.

The temptation was so strong that she had to close her eyes, and a long quiver ran through her. Blair must have been able to feel it, because he withdrew his hand and then slowly lifted his head. When Amanda opened her eyes, she was sure that he must be able to read the naked desire there, but his own expression was indecipherable.

'Ooh, very sexy!' said Nicholas, and as the children all fell about Amanda was able to draw a long breath and step back. God, what was the matter with her? One minute she wanted to punch Blair on the nose and the next she would have given everything she had to be able to put her arms around his neck and melt into him and forget about everything but the feel of his lips and the taste of his mouth.

Still, she *hadn't* given in to the temptation, she tried to reassure herself. Blair probably thought that she had taken it as a quick peck on the cheek, just as he had. That was all it *had* been.

Even so, she found herself ridiculously nervous in case he had misinterpreted that moment when she had trembled in his arms. He was no doubt already convinced that she had hung mistletoe from every available hook in the hope of waylaying him. Amanda cringed at the thought.

She was very much on her dignity for the rest of the day but if Blair noticed, or was impressed by, her coolness he gave no sign of it. 'I'm going to write some cards after I've put the children to bed,' she told him at supper, hoping that he would realise that she had far more important things to do than think about being alone with him.

Blair obviously couldn't have cared less one way or another. 'Fine,' he said. 'I'll be able to get some work done in that case.' And with that he disappeared into his study and Amanda was left struggling to concentrate on a pile of blank Christmas cards. She had always prided herself on including a chatty note with all her cards, but what could she say to her friends in London when they had never met Blair and wouldn't understand how her insides tangled themselves up into a tight knot whenever she remembered each time he had touched her?

She was still conscious of constraint as they set off the next morning. It was the first time she had been in the car with Blair since her arrival, and they should have been able to laugh together over that disastrous journey. Instead they sat and made stilted conversation and pretended that he had never unbuttoned her shirt with his deft fingers, that she had never fallen asleep in his lap and woken to find his fingers twisting through her hair.

It was a relief when Blair finally manoeuvred the big car into a parking space and suggested that they start with the children's presents. 'It's half past eleven already,' he said, checking his watch, 'so we'd better not waste any time.'

In spite of that, they found themselves stopping to listen to a group of carol singers collecting for charity. 'Peace on earth,' said Blair with a twisted smile as they came to the end of 'While Shepherds Watched' and he searched through his pockets for some coins. Failing to find any change, he was forced to hand over a note instead. 'You and I could do with some of that peace on earth, couldn't we, Amanda?'

It was such a relief to know that she wasn't the only one feeling tense and awkward that she could almost feel the rigidity leave her shoulders. 'We've been trying our best,' she reminded him.

'I think we'd better try a bit harder, don't you?' he said, and she smiled almost shyly and nodded.

The last tension between them dissolved when they came across a wonderful toy shop, and Amanda lost all shyness as she rummaged around in a bin of cheap plastic stocking fillers. 'What about this?' she suggested, hooking on a 'disguise' made up of spectacles, a false nose and moustache.

'What about what?' said Blair, turning round and pretending not to notice any change to her face.

'Very funny,' said Amanda as she removed the nose. 'Don't you remember having one of these when you were little? I'm sure Nicholas would love it.'

Blair looked resigned. 'If he did, I'm sure it wouldn't be half as much as you do,' he sighed, but she ignored him.

'I bet he'd like this too,' she giggled, pouncing on a whoopee cushion which let forth a very satisfactory noise. 'And we must get some water-pistols!'

'Must we?' said Blair drily, but he let her toss three into a basket anyway, only drawing the line when it threatened to overflow with exploding soaps and mock creepy-crawlies, along with stickers, models, comics, chocolate money and zany socks. 'There's no need to get carried away,' he told

Amanda, wincing at the contents of the basket. 'Belinda left
some things for their stockings too, and at this rate we're going
to be drowning in plastic! Come and help me choose their
presents instead.'

Amanda rather reluctantly abandoned a squirting camera
and followed Blair over to the sports section where they decided on baseball bats for the boys and, in a different section,
a painting set for Emily. She herself had something rather
more frivolous in mind and let Blair settle up while she found
Emily a tiny plastic house complete with miniature inhabitants
and furniture.

Blair rolled his eyes when he saw it. 'And what on earth
are these?' he said, looking with disbelief at what she had
bought for Simon and Nicholas.

'I'm not sure exactly,' she confided. 'A sort of space-age
weapon, I suppose. But look at the way all the lights flash,
and they make a brilliant noise. Listen.' She demonstrated with
a flourish and he stared at her in appalled disbelief while several shoppers nearby clapped their hands over their ears.

'Amanda, no one in their right mind would introduce a
noise like that into a household at Christmas, let alone double
the volume! We won't be able to hear ourselves think!'

'Oh, well, I expect they'll break after a couple of days,' she
said airily.

Blair sighed. 'Let's hope they break a lot sooner than that!'

They carried all the toys back to the car. 'Do you want to
do some shopping on your own?' he asked her as he relocked
the door.

Amanda, who had been wondering how she was going to
buy Blair a present, seized her chance. 'I do have some presents to get for my family,' she said. 'And I'll need to send off
all these cards.' She flourished those that she had managed to
write the previous night but it was doubtful whether Blair got
the point that she had been much too busy to waste any time
thinking about him.

They arranged to meet in a couple of hours, which left Amanda far too much time to agonise over what to buy him. Why were men always so difficult? So many of the things she looked at just seemed too...intimate, and there didn't seem much point in buying him a book about places he had been when he was in the middle of writing one of his own. In the end she had to admit defeat and settle for a bottle of the whisky that she had drunk so much of the first night they'd met. He could drink this one himself.

It was already getting dark by the time they reached the supermarket on the outskirts of the town. Amanda felt very strange pushing a trolley up and down the aisles with Blair. To anyone else, they must have looked like any other couple, bickering over the shopping list and arguing about which brand of toothpaste to buy. A woman standing next to them at the delicatessen counter overheard Amanda grumbling about the way Blair was objecting to virtually everything she had put on her list, and winked at her sympathetically.

'They *will* interfere, won't they?' she said with a nod at Blair, and Amanda smiled back, grateful for her understanding but uncomfortable at the false impression they were giving. The woman obviously thought they were married.

Did she really *look* like the kind of girl Blair would marry? Amanda wondered half-wistfully. If Blair were her husband they would probably still squabble over the shopping list, but at least she would be able to hang up a bunch of mistletoe without wondering what he would think. She would be able to kiss him out of his bad humour and put her hand on his thigh as they drove home and look forward to spending the evening alone with him without the memory of every time they had touched jangling along her nerves. She wouldn't need to be nervous at all if they were married. She would be accustomed to the feel of his body and the touch of his hands, and his presence would offer the kind of utter security that she had experienced so briefly when his arms had tightened around her on the sledge.

'Amanda!' Blair waved a hand irritably in front of her face and she snapped back to the reality of supermarket shopping with a man who was never likely even to consider marrying her, no matter what passing strangers might think.

'What kind of sausages do you want?' he asked, and with an inward sigh Amanda applied herself to the task in hand.

It seemed to take for ever to get through the checkout with two trolleys piled high with everything they could possibly need and, thanks to Amanda, quite a lot that they probably didn't. By the time they had loaded up the car, she was exhausted, and collapsed back into her seat with a groan.

'I never want to go shopping again!'

'Look on the bright side,' said Blair, inserting the key into the ignition. 'At least we won't starve if we get snowed in.'

He threw his arm along the back of her seat as he looked over his shoulder to reverse out of the parking space, and Amanda felt as if time had slipped, tipping her back to the night she had arrived. Blair had turned then, just as he was turning now, his fingers almost brushing her shoulder and lights throwing shifting shadows over his face. Then he had been a stranger; now he was so familiar that she could have drawn him in her sleep. How could so much have changed in such a short time?

Blair hadn't changed, Amanda decided, studying him under her lashes as he manoeuvred out into the chaotic pre-Christmas traffic. But I have, she admitted silently to herself. If only Blair knew how much!

He drove with the same cool competence with which he did everything else, and for a while Amanda sat looking out at the darkness and wondering how she would ever be able to go back to London. Her life there was like a film she had once seen—vaguely familiar but somehow not real. Reality was

Dundinnie—the cold wind and the children…and Blair. How would she be able to bear leaving them all behind?

Desolation swept over her at the prospect. Until now she hadn't thought beyond Christmas, but Belinda was due back at the beginning of January, and after that there would be no reason for Amanda to stay. Blair would drive her back to the station and put her on the train, no doubt with a sigh of relief, and she would never see any of them again.

Amanda didn't want to know just why the thought was so depressing, and she made a valiant effort to push it away. She was tired and she was hungry, that was all. They had only had time to snatch a quick sandwich at lunchtime and now her stomach rumbled in protest, providing her with a welcome if embarrassing diversion.

'I'm starving,' she said to Blair. 'Can I open those biscuits we bought?'

'Don't tell me you'd be happy with some ginger-nuts?' He pretended to sound astonished, and Amanda knew that he was thinking of how ungrateful she had been when he'd offered her ginger-nuts before. He would never believe that she had really changed.

She sighed. 'They'd be better than nothing.'

'True, but on this occasion we're in a position to fulfil your original fantasy.'

'What?' Amanda goggled at him, wild thoughts of Blair calmly pulling up the car so that he could unbutton her blouse and tilt back the seat and…

'I don't remember the details, but it was something about wine and cheese and sticky toffee pudding.'

Blair's words acted like a dash of cold water and Amanda pulled herself together with an effort, unsure whether to be relieved or disappointed. 'Oh, *that* fantasy,' she said unguardedly.

'Why, which fantasy did you think I was talking about?' he said, amused. 'How many fantasies did you have on that trip?'

Amanda had no intention of telling him *that*. She decided it was wiser to ignore his comment altogether. 'Don't tell me you really can conjure up sticky toffee pudding?' she said, hoping that he didn't notice the betraying squeak in her voice. She cleared her throat and tried to blank out that picture of Blair pulling up the car and turning to her with a smile.

'Not personally,' he said, oblivious to the way her thoughts kept veering out of control. 'But there's a good hotel about thirty miles from here. I vote we stop and have something to eat. I'm hungry too, and we deserve some reward for all that shopping. I'll ring Maggie and tell her that we'll be a bit later.'

The darkness made it seem later than it was and when Amanda glanced across at the clock on the dashboard she was amazed to see that it was not quite half past seven. It was too early for most of the guests to be dining, and as a result they had the vast dining room to themselves. Amanda had to resist the urge to whisper as they discussed the menu.

As soon as she could, she escaped to the Ladies'. It was a much grander hotel than she had been expecting, and she was glad that she had chosen not to wear trousers for a change. It was warm enough indoors to take her jumper off—and the plain white shirt with her soft red skirt looked quite acceptable, she thought as she brushed her hair.

Would Blair think so? Amanda leant towards the mirror to touch up her lipstick and then blotted it all off in case he thought she was making too much of an effort for him.

Compared with the enormous table at the castle, the small polished table for two seemed unbearably intimate, and she was agonisingly conscious of Blair sitting opposite her. It was impossible to avoid looking at him, impossible to stop thinking about that wretched fantasy in the car.

His eyes were lowered as he fingered a knife abstractedly, and she could see the darkness of his lashes and the forceful line of his nose. He was perfectly ordinary, Amanda tried to tell herself desperately. Why couldn't she stop thinking about how it would feel if he kissed her, how warm and sure his hands would be against her skin?

It was at that moment that Blair glanced up, and she stopped breathing. At least, that was what it felt like. It was as if she were suspended above an abyss, motionless for that eternal moment before a dizzying fall into the unknown, held up only by Blair's piercing slate-grey gaze, her own dark and uncertain. She wanted to say something—anything—to break the spell, but she couldn't shape her lips into a word. All she could do was look back at him while the memory of every time he had touched her swirled around her, sucking her down into a churning pit of desire.

The waiter had to speak to them twice before they realised that he was standing right beside them offering a basket of rolls. Amanda took one with shaking fingers and sank limply back into her chair. She had to stop this. Look at Blair, conversing quite normally with the waiter she thought—so cool, so controlled, so patently unmoved. She must have imagined that look, Amanda decided edgily. *His* insides weren't quivering, *his* mind wasn't veering uncontrollably from her mouth to her hands to the feel of her body...

Blair had elected not to drink as he still had some way to drive, but he had insisted that Amanda have a glass of wine. 'I'm still aiming to fulfil that fantasy,' he said with a glimmering smile. 'The one you told me about, anyway.'

That was too close for comfort. She pasted on an over-bright smile and lifted her glass to thank him. 'Consider my fantasies fulfilled!'

'What, all of them?'

Treat it lightly. 'Well, I might keep one or two dreams to myself.'

'Yes, I didn't think you'd be so easily satisfied,' said Blair. His voice was quite neutral but Amanda shot him a suspicious look.

'I suppose that means you've got me down as a *demanding* woman?' Her life in London might seem unreal now, but she hadn't forgotten how difficult it still was for many women to be accepted on equal terms with the men. Women were bossy, men were organised. Men were ambitious, women were demanding. 'We all know how much men hate those!' she said with a hint of remembered irritation.

Blair studied her thoughtfully. 'Maybe I did to begin with,' he said. 'When I first met you, you struck me as someone who knew exactly what she wanted and didn't care what she had to do to get it.'

Amanda quailed inwardly when she remembered how she had ridden roughshod over Sue without giving a thought as to what it might mean to the agency, to Blair or even, more importantly, to the children to have an unprincipled and inexperienced stranger thrust into their midst. She swirled the wine around in her glass without looking at him. 'And now?' she dared to ask.

'Now...now I'm not sure any more.'

'I used to be just like you said,' she blurted out in a burst of confidence. 'I used to be so sure that I knew what I wanted...'

'And now you're not sure either?' Blair finished for her.

'No,' said Amanda, but even as she looked at him she knew that it wasn't true. She *was* sure what she wanted.

She wanted him.

The truth washed over her like a great rolling wave of light—overwhelming, unstoppable, undeniable. Amanda, tumbling helplessly in its wake, found herself swept from exhilaration at the sheer joy of loving him to the bleak bitterness of despair. She couldn't tell Blair that she loved him. She could never have a future with him. It was hopeless. Even if by some miracle he were to love her back, he would soon change his mind when he found out that she had been deceiving him all along.

What if she told him now? It might not be too late, Amanda told herself. She clutched at her wineglass and drew a deep breath. 'Blair?'

He was mindlessly pulling a bread roll apart, looking as if he was trying to make up his mind about something, but when she said his name he glanced up and his gaze was suddenly very alert. 'Yes?'

Amanda opened her mouth to confess that everything she had told him about herself had been a lie, but the words dried in her throat. She couldn't bear to see his face change, to see the expression in his eyes turn to anger and disgust. She would tell him, she vowed, but not now. It would spoil Christmas for everybody, because he would surely send her straight back to London and the children would be disappointed and confused.

Having waited this long, it would be much better to wait until the New Year. When Belinda came back, he wouldn't need her any more, and she would be able to confess, knowing that she had done a good job in spite of her inexperience. And without the children or the need to make Christmas fun for them she would be better able to make Blair understand why she had acted as she had. Yes, it made much more sense to wait.

'Oh...nothing,' she said as she realised that he was still waiting for her to say something. Her eyes slid away from his. 'I've forgotten.'

CHAPTER EIGHT

AN AWKWARD silence fell. They sat facing each other, looking at everything but each other, while the silence stretched until it jangled with tension. Amanda's mind circled frantically in search of something to say, but all she could come up with was, 'I love you,' and she could hardly blurt *that* out without any warning.

In the end it was Blair who spoke first. He cleared his throat. 'I last came here with Bindie.' His voice sounded strained, but Amanda seized on his comment as if it were the most brilliant of conversational starters.

'I wish I had a brother who would take me out to dinner somewhere like this,' she said, forcing gaiety into her voice. 'Mine might buy me a drink in the pub, but that's as far as they would go! You and Belinda must be very close.'

'We are.' Blair seemed to realise that he was still tearing his roll apart and pushed it aside. 'We haven't managed to see each other very often over the last few years—I've been abroad and Bindie's been preoccupied with her family—but that doesn't make any difference. It sounds ridiculous, I know, but I still feel responsible for her.'

He shrugged, half-embarrassed. 'I suppose I got used to looking after her when our parents died, and it's a hard habit to break. And then when Malcolm was killed...well, we were the only ones who really knew how each other felt. Bindie adored Malcolm. I'm sure the only reason she married Paul was because he reminded her of Malcolm. Superficially, he's very like him, but without Malcolm's generosity of spirit.

'The marriage was a disaster from the start,' he went on with a grimace. 'Paul could never be Malcolm, and anyway,

132

Bindie really needs someone steady and reliable who'll cosset her and look after her, not someone with that kind of mercurial temperament. She put up with his affairs for years for the sake of the children, and in the end it was Paul who walked out. He said he was bored with family life, but it hasn't stopped him turning round and marrying one of his colleagues and starting a family with *her*.'

'Was Belinda very upset?'

'To be honest, I think it knocked her confidence more than anything else. She hadn't been in love with Paul for a long time, but I suppose she was used to being there for him. I'm hoping that these few weeks in New Zealand will have given her a fresh start.'

Amanda watched him, thinking of the way he cared for his sister, of how, one day, he might care for a wife. 'You're a good brother,' she said softly.

For a brief moment his eyes met hers, and she felt her heart contract with the longing to reach out and touch his hand. She picked up her glass rather unsteadily instead. 'What about Malcolm?' she asked in a voice that sounded higher than usual. Anything to break the silence. 'Was he married?'

'He was engaged,' said Blair flatly.

'Didn't you like his fiancée?'

'Oh, I liked her all right.' This time there was no mistaking the bitterness. 'I liked her so much that I was engaged to her as well.'

Amanda remembered what Maggie had told her about Iona with her long, beautiful hair, but surely she hadn't said anything about Malcolm? 'That must have been a bit awkward,' she said feebly.

'That's one way of putting it,' said Blair with grim humour. 'Particularly as we were both engaged to her at the same time, although that was a little detail Iona preferred to keep to herself.'

'But how did she keep you apart?' asked Amanda, who

couldn't understand why Iona would have wanted anyone else when she'd already had Blair.

'Oh, that was easy. I, poor trusting fool that I was, had gone off to Brazil for six months. It never occurred to me that Iona wasn't doing exactly what she'd said she was doing in her letters, which was missing me, longing for my return and all the other things people in love are supposed to do.'

Amanda thought bleakly about how *she* was going to miss him. Iona hadn't known how lucky she was. At least she had had the prospect of Blair returning. 'So you met her first?'

'I met her at a party in Edinburgh.' Blair's mouth twisted in wry memory. 'It was quite something to be a McAllister of Dundinnie then, or at least Iona thought so. I was young, and bowled over by her beauty, and in no time at all we were engaged. I was so proud of her,' he remembered bitterly. 'I couldn't wait to take her to Dundinnie and show her off to my uncle and aunt, and Iona played the part of the sweet bride-to-be to perfection, except that while she was there she learnt that I was only the nephew and that Malcolm was heir to Dundinnie.'

He stopped and shook his head, as if amazed at his own stupidity. 'Dundinnie was worth quite a lot in those days, and the poor relation was obviously not what Iona had in mind at all. The next thing I knew, she was talking about going to London while I was in Brazil. I gave her Malcolm's address, I even told her to get in touch with him as I badly wanted him to approve of my choice, but I didn't get a chance to introduce them myself as I had to leave earlier than planned. I wasn't in the kind of places you could get a letter, so I didn't hear from Iona for six months. That was all right—I thought I'd surprise her by turning up unexpectedly.' He laughed without humour.

Amanda had been listening with a kind of horrified fascination. 'Was she with Malcolm when you arrived?'

'Oh, nothing that dramatic,' said Blair sardonically. 'I'd

moved hell and high water to fly home early so that I could get to a surprise family reunion my aunt and Belinda had arranged for my uncle at Dundinnie. I rang Iona, of course, from Rio, but she wasn't in, so I had to leave a message on her machine. She wasn't at the airport either, and although I was bitterly disappointed I just assumed that she was away and that it was my fault for not letting her know earlier.'

'So what happened?' asked Amanda, not even sure that she wanted to know.

'I came straight on up to Dundinnie for the party. Malcolm was there.' Blair gave another twisted smile. 'He wasn't a great one for keeping in touch. He hadn't even heard that I was engaged, but he was delighted for me, especially as he too had just decided to get married. He hadn't brought his fiancée up because he'd wanted my uncle to be the centre of attention, but he was sure we would all love her. He'd brought a photograph to show us.'

Amanda bit her lip, able to imagine only too vividly what Blair's feelings must have been when he'd looked at that photograph. 'So he *had* met her?'

'Oh, yes, Iona had made sure of that. She'd set her heart on Dundinnie, and she'd seduced Malcolm utterly, just as she'd seduced me. You'd have to see her to know how beautiful she was,' Blair tried to explain. 'No man could have resisted her, but Malcolm would have tried his damnedest if he'd known that she was supposed to be mine. He was that sort of man. As it was, he was devastated when he realised the truth.'

'As you must have been.'

He acknowledged her comment with what might have been a smile. 'I wasn't exactly thinking clearly, it's true, but Malcolm took it particularly badly. He kept saying that there must have been some mistake, and before I realised what he intended to do he had driven back down to London to confront Iona and ask her if it was true.'

'What did she say?'

'She lied,' said Blair tightly. 'She admitted that she knew me, but she told him that she'd never said that she loved me. She claimed that I was a mere boy and that our engagement had just been wishful thinking on my part.'

Amanda found that her fingers were curled into tight fists and forced herself to relax them. 'He didn't believe her?'

'No, he didn't believe her. He knew me, and he believed me, although it cost him everything to do it. He rang me in a terrible state, saying that he'd broken everything off with Iona and that all he wanted was to come home to Dundinnie.' Blair looked across at Amanda, his expression bleak. 'He never made it home.'

Amanda lifted her hand to her mouth in an unconscious gesture of horror as he went on. 'He was killed on the way. He should never have been driving in the condition he was in, and it was a mercy that no one else was involved, but that wasn't much consolation to my uncle and aunt. My uncle had a stroke immediately after Malcolm's funeral, and he died five days later. My aunt died the following year. They say people don't really die of a broken heart, but she did.'

'I'm so sorry,' said Amanda quietly, wishing she could put her arms around him. 'It must have been ghastly for you.'

Blair managed to raise a smile. 'Well, at least I'm not a target for fortune-hunting girls any more. Inheritance tax took care of Dundinnie's assets and ensured that in future any girl will have to love me for what I am.'

He was trying to joke, but Amanda wanted to cry, I do! Instead she asked what had happened to Iona, and his face hardened.

'She didn't dare come to the funeral. She knew she would have to face me, and that I knew that she'd killed Malcolm as surely as if she had put a gun to his head. She would have said that she hadn't done anything, but, as far as I'm concerned, her lies killed three people that I loved dearly. I'll never be able to forgive her for that.'

Liar, liar, liar. Amanda made herself repeat the ugly word in her head as they drove the last half-hour back to Dundinnie. What right did she have to judge Iona? She too was a liar, and when he found out Blair would never forgive her either.

But it wasn't the same, she tried to persuade herself. Her lies were harmless compared with Iona's. Surely as long as she told him herself that she had lied he wouldn't compare her to Iona? He would realise that she was different, that when she said she loved him she was speaking only the truth.

Blair too was silent, no doubt reliving the horrible events of the past. Having watched his face as he'd told her the story, Amanda was more than ever convinced that she was right to put off telling him about her own deceit. Blair and the children deserved a happy Christmas and she was going to do everything in her power to make sure that they had one.

A gleam of yellow light showed between the sitting-room curtains as Blair parked the car on the gravel outside the great wooden door. Staggering slightly under the weight, Amanda put down her load of carrier bags on the step and flexed her fingers as Blair searched through his pockets for the key. It was only now that she realised how tired she was, and she leant wearily back against the wall and closed her eyes for a moment.

When she opened them, Blair had the key in his hand but was making no attempt to open the door. Instead he was staring at her as if he had never seen her before. Amanda felt as if there was an electric current surging between them, and she straightened with a questioning look.

Their eyes met in the blurry light of the outside lamp, and Blair took a step towards her. 'Amanda—' he began, his voice an odd mixture of urgency and uncertainty, and her heart began to slam against her ribs, but before he could say any more the door was thrown open and light from the hall flooded over them.

'I thought I heard a car,' said Maggie's comfortable voice, and then she stopped as she saw the way Blair and Amanda were blinking in the light as if they had been jerked out of a dream. 'Is something the matter?'

'No,' said Blair. 'No,' he said again, more firmly this time. 'Have the kids been all right?'

'No, we haven't!' said Simon, appearing in the doorway before Maggie could answer. 'We've got a crisis!'

'What's happened?' asked Blair sharply as Amanda took an involuntary step forward. 'Is it serious?'

'Serious? It's a disaster! Your rotten television has broken and we'll never be able to get it fixed in time for Christmas!'

When Amanda woke late the next morning, the strange light and muffled quietness told her that it had been snowing before she even opened the curtains. Even so, she was unprepared at how deep it lay already.

'It's just as well we went to town yesterday,' said Blair, stamping the snow off his boots as he brought in more logs for the fire. 'I only just got Maggie home in time last night.'

'Do you think it's set in?' The knowledge of how much she loved him had made Amanda shy of Blair this morning, and after the emotions of last night she was glad to keep the conversation to the weather.

'I do. It looks like we'll get a white Christmas after all.'

The news went some way to consoling the children for the loss of the television. Once they had accepted that Blair had no intention of repeating the previous day's drive to buy a replacement, they threw themselves into Amanda's suggestion that they produce their own play instead.

'That was a stroke of genius,' Blair said admiringly as they disappeared importantly after lunch. 'I was ready to crown the next one who complained about all the films they were going to miss!'

The smile that went with his words of praise kept Amanda warm all afternoon. She watched the snowflakes flurry past the windows and hugged the knowledge of their isolation to herself. In spite of the draughty corridors and the echoing stone walls, the castle seemed cosy, a refuge from the outside world. Maggie had obviously spent the day defying Blair's express orders that she should not do any cooking and had left tins of mince pies and pots of warming soups, as well as a selection of cakes and pies for the freezer. They had plenty of food after yesterday's shopping marathon; they had fires for warmth and each other for company. Amanda wanted to stay snowed in for ever.

Blair had abandoned his book until Christmas was over, and in the evenings they gathered round the fire in the sitting room and played all the games that Amanda hadn't played since she'd been a child. They had always involved a lot of shouting and squabbling in her day too and she was relieved to see that nothing had changed. Blair expanded their repertoire of card games too, although the children loyally maintained that the poker which Amanda had taught them was their favourite. They made Blair play as well, until they realised that he was the only one able to keep a straight face and always ended up winning.

They had refused to divulge anything about the play, which was apparently going to be a major production, and which occupied most of the next three days, but by Christmas Eve they declared that it was ready and that Amanda and Blair were formally invited as an audience. Two chairs had been set facing the 'stage' which was cluttered with an assortment of scenery. Amanda felt quite choked when she saw how much trouble they had been to. There was even a programme, complete with an extraordinarily long cast list, and a cassette player had been set up to provide incidental music. Nicholas was evidently in charge of this, because he kept disappearing off-stage in the middle of a scene to switch it on and off.

Blair handed Amanda a glass of mulled wine as he slipped into the seat beside hers. 'I think we might need this!' he said in an undertone.

He had a jug at his feet, and kept filling up their glasses during the endless scene changes. Whether it was the wine or the happiness of having him next to her, Amanda thought the play was the funniest thing she had ever seen. The plot was so complicated that Blair had to give her a running commentary under his breath, and they both laughed so much that they had to wipe the tears from their eyes, while the children waited in pitying and disapproving silence for them to finish so that they could continue.

Afterwards, as it was Christmas Eve, they lit the candles on the tree in the sitting room and Amanda insisted that they sing carols. To her astonishment, Blair announced that he used to be able to play the piano, so they dragged it out of its corner and he sat down to run his fingers experimentally over the keys. It was rather out of tune and Blair's playing decidedly rusty, but when it got too painful Amanda and the children just sang louder to drown it out. They romped through all the favourites, and then Emily sang 'Away in a Manger' by herself, and Amanda felt her eyes sting with emotion.

The children were wildly excited all evening. It took ages to persuade them to bed that night, and Blair and Amanda still had presents to wrap and stockings to fill. Since their shopping trip together they had, by unspoken agreement, spent as little time alone together as possible. When the children were there, they seemed to be able to act perfectly naturally, but on their own both were conscious of an unacknowledged tension.

That night, tension or no tension, there was work to be done. Blair provided three long socks and Amanda stuffed them from the piles she had sorted out, not forgetting the obligatory tangerine in each toe. They all looked satisfactorily lumpy and exciting when she had finished, and she remembered her own childhood with a pang. Few things would ever match that indescribable moment when you woke up and felt the weight of a Christmas stocking against your feet.

'It's a bit late to tell me that you'd like a stocking now!' said Blair when she told him as much.

'The trouble with growing up is that a stocking wouldn't give you the same wonderful feeling any more,' she said rather sadly.

'True,' he said, 'but other feelings are just as wonderful when you grow up. I can think of a lot more exciting things to do than wake up with a stocking!'

He was teasing her, Amanda realised, even as she thought that she too could think of more exciting moments. Waking up with Blair would be more wonderful than a hundred stockings strewn across her bed.

She had tried hard not to think too much about loving him over the last three days. Alone in bed she had let herself imagine that everything would work out, that she would never have to confess to being an impostor, that Blair would sweep her up into his arms and refuse to let her go back to London. During the day it was harder to forget the reality of her own deception, and almost everything she did made her achingly aware of what she would never have. So often they seemed on the surface like a real family, chasing each other through the snow and tumbling home to tea around the fire, and Amanda's heart would tighten painfully at the knowledge that she and Blair would never have a family, would never have Christmas together again.

Times like this were bitter-sweet. Amanda watched Blair wrapping up Emily's painting set with characteristic efficiency, loving the fact that he was near and that she could watch the way the fire threw flickering shadows over his face, but torn by the impossibility of her dreams. She shouldn't let herself imagine what it would be like if they were married and

wrapping presents for children of their own, she told herself.
That way lay despair. Instead, she would just make the most
of the times they had, like now, when the constraint between
them had melted in the firelight and the only sounds were the
ticking of the clock and the occasional splutter as a log crumbled into the hot coals.

Blair set the last present under the tree and glanced at his
watch, yawning. 'Do you think it's time to play Father
Christmas yet?'

'Do you want me to go and see if they're asleep?'

'No, I'll go,' he said, getting to his feet. 'You stay here by
the fire.'

Amanda sat on the rug and stared into the flames, so absorbed in her thoughts of Blair and what could never be that
she didn't realise at first that he had come back and was standing near the door watching the shadows play over her still
figure. They had switched off the overhead light and it was
impossible to read his expression.

'Amanda?' he said softly, and she started, jerked out of a
beatific dream in which they were wrapping presents until he
calmly leant across and took the scissors from her hand so that
he could draw her down onto the hearth-rug with him…

'Are…are they asleep?' she asked, appalled at the squeak
in her voice.

'Dead to the world.' Blair moved forward out of the shadows and reached down a hand to help her to her feet. 'Come
with me. I want to show you something.'

His fingers were warm and strong as they closed around
hers, and Amanda had to force herself to let them go once she
was standing. 'What is it?'

'Wait and see.'

He led her across the hall and opened the door quietly.
'Look.'

Amanda looked. Some time during the evening it must have
stopped snowing, and the sky was brilliant with stars. They

shimmered down on the snow that lay in a soft, pristine mantle over everything. It was utterly quiet and still.

'"Silent night, holy night."' She whispered the words of the carol they had sung earlier that evening.

Blair nodded. 'It's midnight,' he said softly. 'Happy Christmas.'

Amanda felt her throat tighten with unaccountable tears. 'Happy Christmas,' she said in a husky voice. She felt as if she had never understood the real meaning of Christmas before now, looking out onto the starlit snow with Blair beside her and their breath hanging in frozen clouds.

The silence enveloped them as they stood and watched, oblivious of the cold. Amanda was never sure at what point she stopped being awed by the beauty of the night and began being aware of the fact that Blair was only inches away and that a single step would be enough to let her lean against him. The urge to do just that was so strong that she forced herself to turn, terrified that unless she moved she would simply curl herself around him like bindweed.

She stopped dead as she noticed the mistletoe hanging from the doorway for the first time. 'Who put that there?' she asked involuntarily.

'Who put what—?' Following her gaze, Blair glanced up the mistletoe that dangled just above his head. 'I've no idea,' he said in an odd voice. 'But I appear to be standing right beneath it.'

Amanda's heart slowed to a painful thump. 'Does that mean I have to kiss you?' She tried to sound as if she was joking, but she could hear the crack in her voice.

'Only if you want to,' said Blair.

Their eyes met in the frosty air, and all at once Amanda felt her doubts dissolve into the single certainty that for tonight she didn't need to pretend any more. All she needed to do was take that step.

Very slowly, she stepped towards him so that she could rest

her hands on his broad shoulders. 'I do,' she said, looking up at him.

Blair didn't move, but she could feel him tense, and she remembered how he had promised not to lay a finger on her unless she specifically invited him. Now, at last, she could issue that invitation. For a long moment she just stood there, savouring the feel of his shoulders beneath her fingers and the delicious anticipation of knowing that she could kiss him whenever she wanted to, and then she slid her hands slowly round his neck so that she could pull his head down until their lips were almost touching.

'Happy Christmas, Blair,' she murmured, and pressed her mouth to his in a kiss that was warm and long and achingly sweet.

When it was over, Blair raised his head long enough to whisper an unsteady, 'Happy Christmas,' in return before he took her up on her invitation and gathered her back into his arms at last.

In that moment as his lips came down on hers, Christmas, the starlit night and the bitter cold were all blotted out by a wave of inexpressible delight. Amanda melted into his kiss, giddy with relief and the sheer joy of being able to kiss him back the way she had dreamt about doing for so long.

His mouth was so warm, so exciting, and the feel of his arms around her filled her with a pleasure so intense that it hurt. At last she could lean into the hardness of his body. She could spread her hands over his back and revel in the feel and the touch and the taste of him while the kiss went on and on and gloriously on.

'Amanda...' Blair murmured her name breathlessly at last, kissing his way along her jawline. He twined his fingers in her shining hair, and she tipped her head back, shivering with delight at the feel of his lips against the sensitive pulse that beat just below her ear. 'Amanda, I've wanted to kiss you like this ever since that damned doctor brought you home.'

Amanda was kissing his throat, breathing in the scent of his skin. 'Why didn't you?' she mumbled.

'I promised I wouldn't,' said Blair virtuously. 'I can't tell you how many times I regretted it, but you didn't seem very keen on the idea at the time.'

'I changed my mind,' she said, and he kissed her again.

Some time later, she drew a ragged sigh of pure happiness and leant into him so that he could wrap his arms tightly around her and rest his cheek against her hair. 'You put that mistletoe up there, didn't you?' she teased, and felt Blair smile.

'It's corny, I know,' he admitted, 'but it was the best I could think of at the time. I didn't think I could get through Christmas Day without kissing you, and you'd been so insistent that I wasn't to touch you until you asked that I thought the only thing I could do was to try and get you to kiss me first.'

'And it worked,' she sighed happily. 'You must have known that it would.'

'No, I didn't know,' said Blair, suddenly serious. 'I just hoped.' He cupped her face between his strong brown hands and looked down into her eyes. 'Amanda, I'd like to take you to bed and make love to you all night, but I have a horrible vision of three excited children erupting into the room at some unearthly hour of the morning, and we don't want anything to spoil our first time together, do we?'

'No, we don't...but perhaps if they're up early they'll be so tired by the evening that they'll be ready for an early night?'

Blair smiled, not fooled for a moment by her innocent air. 'That's what I'm counting on!' he said, and they exchanged a kiss that was warm with promise. 'I suppose if we're going to be up early, we'd better get some sleep as well,' he said reluctantly at last, but without letting her go.

It was Amanda who eased herself out of his arms with a sigh. 'You've still got a job to do,' she reminded him, soft-

ening her words with a final kiss. 'Come on, Santa, it's time
you did your stuff.'

It was still dark when Amanda woke up on Christmas morning, but she felt as if she was drenched in sunlight. For a
moment she lay, conscious only of the happiness seeping
through her, and then the door opened, and Emily was clam-
bering onto her bed, closely followed by Nicholas and Simon,
all in their pyjamas and all looking distinctly rumpled.

'We wanted to open our stockings with you, and we've been
waiting ages and ages,' said Emily in a rush. 'And Uncle Blair
wouldn't let us wake you, but you're awake, aren't you?'

Amanda laughed and stretched so that the happiness tingled
right down to her fingertips. 'I am now!'

Blair came into the room, holding a bottle of champagne
and two glasses, as she was pulling herself up onto her pillows
and at once the indefinable sense of contentment focused into
an electrifying jolt of sheer joy. Like the children, he looked
as if he had just rolled out of bed. He hadn't yet shaved, his
stubble gave him a vaguely rakish air, and he had plainly
pulled on the first clothes that had come to hand, but Amanda
thought he looked wonderful.

'Champagne!' Relaxing back into her pillows, she smiled
at him over the children's heads and was rewarded by the
expression in his eyes as he set the glasses down on the chest
of drawers. How could she ever have thought that his eyes
were cold? This morning they were more blue than grey, and
their warmth was a caress that melted her heart.

'You did order it some time ago,' he reminded her, 'so I
didn't dare not produce a bottle, but I can bring you a cup of
tea if you'd prefer.'

'Oh, no!' said Amanda, watching him deftly unwrap the
gold foil and ease the cork out of the bottle. 'This is definitely
a morning for champagne!'

'Here you are.' Blair presented her glass with a flourish,

and as she took it with a smile that was meant just for him he leant down and kissed her on the cheek, the roughness of his skin grazing hers tantalisingly. 'Happy Christmas, Amanda.'

'Happy Christmas,' she said demurely, as if they hadn't already exchanged the same greeting much more passionately a few hours earlier.

Straightening, Blair found himself being stared at by three pairs of eyes. 'What are you lot looking at?' he said with mock gruffness.

'You kissed Amanda!' said Nicholas accusingly, and Emily giggled into her hand.

'It's Christmas,' said Blair. 'It's allowed. Isn't it, Amanda?'

'Definitely,' said Amanda.

Simon looked up from his stocking. 'Why do you keep smiling at each other like that?' he demanded.

'Like what?'

'Like we weren't here.'

Instinctively, Blair's eyes met Amanda's and they exchanged a rueful smile.

'Like *that*!' said Simon in disgust.

'Sorry.' Blair assumed a humble expression. 'I won't do it again. And you're not to smile either, Amanda! It's Christmas Day; you're not supposed to be smiling! When you look at me, you're to frown like this.' He screwed up his face into a horrible grimace, and Amanda managed a ferocious look in return which made the children giggle and successfully turned the subject as they vied with each other as to who could pull the most hideous face before they went back to the really important business of digging into their stockings to see what else they could find.

When the sun came up, it revealed a sparkling morning. It was so cold that it hurt to breathe and they had to narrow their eyes against the glitter of the snow. Belinda rang from New Zealand, and although the children's control wobbled a bit at the sound of their mother's voice the news that her friend had recovered so well that she would be able to come home earlier than she had thought was enough to cheer them up again.

Knowing how much they had missed their mother without making a fuss about it, Amanda felt guilty that she was dreading Belinda's return, when she would have to make a clean breast of everything to Blair. A chill touched her at the thought that they might only have less than another week together, but she refused to let anything spoil this perfect day.

There was no question of getting out to the road, let alone to church, so after breakfast Blair and Amanda succumbed to the children's frenzied impatience and agreed that it was time to open the presents under the tree. All was chaos for a while, and Amanda was very glad of their excitement with their own parcels, for it meant that none of them noticed her reaction when she opened her present from Blair.

He had given her a topaz necklace so beautiful that at first she could only stare at it, overwhelmed. It hung around her neck all day, warm and heavy, and she kept fingering it with incredulous delight. Every time she touched it, she thrilled with the knowledge that Blair had chosen it for her, and it seemed charged both with the memory of the way he had kissed her and the promise of the night to come.

When all the presents had been gloated over and the wrapping paper tidied away, Blair tried his best to tire them all out by dragging them out for a walk, but the snow was so deep that they ended up sinking above their knees and it soon degenerated into a snowball fight. Completely over-excited by then, they galloped back to Dundinnie, where, just as Blair had predicted, Amanda was soon heartily sick of the sound of the space-age guns she had given Nicholas and Simon.

They had decided to have the meal early in the evening, and she was contemplating cooking her first roast turkey with all the trimmings with some trepidation, but Blair and the children dealt with all the vegetables, and if the gravy was a little lumpy then no one was in the mood to complain. Afterwards, they played games, although the children were quick to notice that neither Blair nor Amanda appeared to be concentrating.

Both were, in fact, alert for the first yawn, but in the end Blair was forced to suggest that they could all do with an early night. They made token protests, of course, but didn't put up too much of a fight. When Amanda went up to say goodnight, they were all waiting for her in Emily's room.

'We just wanted to say thank you for Christmas,' said Simon gruffly. 'We thought it was going to be awful without Mum, but you made it fun.'

Tears stung Amanda's eyes. 'You made it fun for me too,' she said, thinking that she was going to miss them almost as much as she was Blair.

Emily gave her extra Christmas kisses once she was tucked up in bed. The boys had made it very clear that they were too old for kissing, but when Amanda went into the next room to turn out their light they both hugged her tightly. Terrified of embarrassing them by crying, Amanda wished them a husky goodnight, but her heart was full as she closed their door behind her and went downstairs to Blair.

Having waited all day for this moment, she was suddenly— stupidly—shy. The door to the sitting room was ajar, and she hesitated outside before taking a deep breath and slipping inside. Blair was standing by the fire, waiting for her. For a moment they looked across the room at each other, as if neither was certain whether to make the first move or not, then he smiled.

'Come here,' he said, and opened his arms.

CHAPTER NINE

AMANDA walked straight into them, her shyness dissolving as they closed around her.

'I've been wanting to do this all day,' sighed Blair, kissing her eyes, her cheeks, her mouth. He sank down in the big old armchair and pulled her onto his lap, and Amanda wound her arms around his neck so that she could melt into him, kiss after deep, hungry kiss.

'Thank you for my beautiful necklace,' she murmured into his ear, aeons later.

'Do you like it?'

'I love it,' she said, meaning I love you.

Blair lifted the necklace so that the warm stones ran through his fingers, glimmering in the firelight. 'As soon as I saw this, I thought of you. It's exactly the colour of your eyes when you're smiling.'

'That's funny,' said Amanda. 'As soon as I saw the whisky, I thought of *you*. I thought it might remind you of the first night we spent together.'

'Everything reminds me of that night,' he said softly, beginning to press slow, sensuous kisses against her throat. 'Every time you turn your head, or smile, I think about how much I want to spend another night with you.' His voice was muffled against her warm skin. 'Every time I see you in a shirt, I think about unbuttoning it the way I did that night. I think about sliding it down from your shoulders and letting it drop to the floor.'

Amanda shivered with delicious anticipation. In honour of Christmas dinner, she was wearing a softly pleated chocolate-brown skirt with an ivory tunic that had been one of her most extravagant purchases. Luxuriously made of double silk, it had a simple round neck and lots of tiny buttons, each fastened with a loop of material at the front, and she had draped a heavy gold silk shawl around her shoulders as an extra layer.

Blair was pulling one end now so that it slithered in a silken mass down her arm and whispered into a heap on the floor. 'I haven't been able to concentrate on anything else all evening,' he confessed. 'I kept getting distracted by the way you looked tonight. I'd be trying to play a game with the children, and all I could do was wonder if this moment would ever come, whether I would start to undo these buttons at the bottom or the top.'

His hand slid tantalisingly back up over the silk to her neck-line and all the air leaked out of Amanda's lungs. 'What did you decide?' she asked in a cracked whisper.

'I thought I'd start at the top,' said Blair with a smile that melted her bones. Very slowly, very surely, he began to un-fasten the loops of material, his fingers moving steadily from button to button while every nerve in Amanda's body strummed with exquisite anticipation. He was barely touching her, and already she felt ready to shatter with excitement.

The last fastening fell apart. Amanda held her breath as Blair lifted his eyes to smile at her once more before he slid his hand beneath the silk. The feel of it made her gasp, and she closed her eyes against the stab of desire. 'D-do you think the children are asleep yet?' she said with difficulty.

Blair's hand was drifting up to her breast. 'I do hope so,' he murmured into her throat. 'Shall we go upstairs and see?'

Tipping her gently off his knee, he took her hand then led her up the sweeping staircase. Outside the sitting room, the air was glacial, but Amanda didn't notice. She was burning, so weak with longing that she could hardly put one foot in front of the other, and it was all she could do to stay upright as she leant helplessly against the wall while Blair checked on the children.

'Fathoms deep,' he reported. He tugged Amanda away from the wall and she went unresisting into his arms once more. 'I think it's time we went to bed too, don't you?' he said quietly, and, when she nodded, drew her further down the corridor to his room.

He shouldered open the door and pulled Amanda inside. There was a single lamp burning by the bed, but she didn't think she could make it that far. Instead she collapsed back against the door, taking Blair with her as they kissed with an increasing urgency, their hands moving hungrily over each other.

Reaching round her, Blair unzipped her skirt and it puddled unnoticed at her feet while he pushed aside the silk top and let his lips follow the heart-stopping exploration of his hands. Amanda tipped back her head, incoherent with desire, unsure whether she was exhilarated or terrified by the spinning sensations his every touch evoked. She had never felt like this before, never burned with such hunger.

His mouth was at her breast, warm and insistent, and he held her secure between his hard hands as he sank to his knees, searing kisses down to the satiny skin of her stomach until she cried out. Twisting her fingers in his dark hair, Amanda arched against him and he eased down her pants so that he could run his hands back up the smooth length of her legs, letting them drift possessively over her thighs and the soft sweep of her hip while his lips scorched a trail back up to her breasts once more, and the silk top slithered unnoticed off her shoulders.

'Amanda…' Blair's voice was ragged as he pressed her back against the door with the weight of his body and they exchanged deep, almost desperate kisses. Amanda tugged his shirt from his trousers, but her fingers were too unsteady to unbutton it, and in the end it was Blair who wrenched it off. At last she was able to run her hands over his bare chest and savour the taste and texture of his skin.

'Shall we make ourselves more comfortable?' said Blair a

little shakily, and although she was reluctant to let him go for even a second Amanda let herself be pulled across the room. Her eyes were wide and dark as she watched him discard the rest of his clothes. In the lamplight, his lean, muscled body had a strength and a sheen that stopped the breath in her throat, and she felt her bones dissolve with longing.

He reached for her then, drawing her down with him onto the wide bed, and for Amanda time ceased to exist. With the first unimpeded meeting of their bodies, her senses seemed to take on an extra dimension and she was sucked unresisting into a swirling vortex of desire. Nothing mattered but Blair's hands and Blair's mouth and the sleek, steely strength of the body possessing hers with such mastery. Wrapping herself around him, she let him guide her through the tumbling, turbulent rush of feelings, each breaking over the last and pushing them up and up in a wild surge of passion that was frightening in its intensity and power.

'Blair...Blair...' Amanda sobbed his name, terrified that he would let her go, and he murmured a reassurance as the timeless rhythm bore them up above the whirling emotions at last into the blinding light. For an eternity they paused there, and then the light exploded into a million shimmering pieces and they spun helplessly down through them until suddenly they were back on the bed, still dazzled and blinking at the return to reality.

Amanda felt as if she had dropped through a time-warp. Blair lay on top of her, breathing heavily, his face pressed into her neck, his warmth and his weight infinitely reassuring. For a long while, they simply lay entwined while the golden glow of fulfilment seeped through them, dissolving Amanda's bones into molten honey and brimming over into every pore.

Mellow with enchantment, she ran her hands lovingly over Blair's broad shoulders and he stirred and mumbled kisses and endearments into her throat before raising himself up on one elbow to look down into her face. The bright brown eyes were glowing, and her mouth was curved into a smile of sheer contentment. Tenderly, he smoothed the silky brown hair away from her face.

'You're beautiful,' he said softly, and gathered her to him as he rolled over onto his back.

Amanda lay contentedly against his shoulder while he let his hand drift absently over her curves. She wanted no more than this—to breathe in the scent of his skin and listen to the steady beat of his heart, to feel the hard security of his body close to hers and remember the astounding joy they had discovered together. There was no need to talk about love or worry about the future; his arms were around her, her lips were still warm from his kiss and for now that was enough.

The enchantment stayed with Amanda for the days that followed. Sometimes she would look at Blair and her heart would clench with the need to reach out and touch him. It was hard now to believe that she had once thought him cold. The stern mouth had relaxed and the laughter lines that creased the edges of his eyes were very pronounced. He looked younger and happier than Amanda had ever thought possible, and she thrilled at the knowledge that it was because of her.

They were careful not to touch each other during the day. Amanda was growing increasingly fond of the children, but she counted the hours until they were in bed and she could melt into Blair's arms. He never said that he loved her, but all he had to do was kiss her and Amanda knew that it was true. Neither of them felt the need to talk about the future when all that mattered was the present and the long, sweet hours when they were alone.

For Amanda, the memory of those three days remained forever golden, although later she was unable to say exactly what they did. All she remembered was the sunlight sparkling on the snow and the breathtaking passion that she and Blair discovered in each other every night. They were adrift in their own world, isolated by the snowdrifts, cut off from time and reality.

It was a world that ended on December the twenty-ninth when the thaw set in and Norris Jeffries rang. Amanda had forgotten all about her promise to ring him, and so was unprepared when Blair came into kitchen looking boot-faced.

'There's a phone call for you,' he said stiffly.

'For me?' Amanda put down the teatowel she had been using to dry the lunch dishes. 'Who is it?' she added without thinking, although even as she was speaking she was remembering Norris and his ultimatum. The end of December, he had said, and now her time was up.

'He said he was a "friend",' said Blair with distaste, managing to put inverted commas around the word. 'I didn't think it would be tactful to enquire any further.'

Amanda's heart sank at his expression. Surely he couldn't be jealous of Norris? But how could she reassure him without telling him the truth?

Even as she hesitated, Blair was turning abruptly away. 'You'd better go,' he said. 'He sounded very anxious to speak to you.'

Chilled by his sudden change of attitude, Amanda went slowly up to the study and picked up the phone. Norris never wasted any time on preliminaries. 'Well? How's the big seduction going?' he asked crudely.

Amanda closed her eyes. At the time it had seemed a good ploy to let Norris think that she was trying to seduce Blair for the sake of the deal, but now she felt physically sick at the idea. It was too late to change things now, though, and all she had to do was buy enough time to let her make her own confession to Blair. Gritting her teeth, she told him that everything was going to plan.

'Does that mean you've got an agreement?'

'I think I've persuaded him to think about your offer,' she said after a moment.

Norris was unimpressed. 'Is that all? You should have had him eating out of your hand by now!'

'I just need a few more days,' said Amanda desperately. 'Once I start talking about leaving, he'll do anything to keep me.'

'I'll give you another week,' he said, and put down the phone.

Amanda replaced the receiver more slowly. Her enchanted world was dissolving as surely as the snow dripping steadily off the roof. Belinda was coming home the next day, and once the excitement was over she would have to sit down and talk with Blair. Nothing would be the same after that.

Nothing was the same now, she thought bleakly, remembering Blair's expression when he'd told her about the phone call. She would have to try and explain so that nothing spoilt what might be their last night.

But when she went to look for Blair he had disappeared. He spent the afternoon shovelling snow out of the driveway and only came in when it started to get dark. Amanda was dismayed to see that that the shuttered look had returned to his face.

'That was just a friend on the phone,' she tried to explain, but Blair only looked disbelieving.

'*Just* a friend?' he echoed. 'He must be a very good friend if you gave him your number here.'

'Well, he…he is,' stammered Amanda. 'But he's not a boy-friend or anything,' she added quickly.

'You don't need to explain anything,' said Blair so coldly that her heart cracked. It was as if the warm, loving man had suddenly become a stranger. Only he wasn't a complete stranger: this was the Blair who had met her off the train, the Blair she thought had vanished entirely. 'Your life in London is nothing to do with me.'

Amanda felt as if he had slapped her. He could hardly have made it clearer that he expected her to go back to that life, and that he would have no part in it. 'No, I suppose it isn't,' she said with a brittle smile.

She had been living in a dream world, Amanda realised bitterly. She had been so sure that he loved her, so certain that he hadn't said it only because there had been no need to say it, but perhaps after all he had just made love to her because she was there and because they were alone.

Amanda couldn't believe how one phone call could spoil everything. It wasn't even as if they had had a blazing row, but somehow Blair seemed to have retreated and she was too miserably conscious of how she had lied to be able to put things right. If she had been able to explain about Norris, it might have been different, but how could she confess when Blair wouldn't even listen to her?

For the first time since Christmas, Amanda slept alone in her room. Her bed was cold and empty, and she ached for the comfort of Blair's body. She lay awake for hours, waiting for his footsteps, imagining him walking softly across the room and sliding into bed beside her. He would take her in his arms and tell her that he had just been jealous, that he didn't want her to go, and then, when they were lying close together, she would tell him about Norris and he would say that it didn't matter. Nothing mattered as long as they were together.

But Blair didn't come. He let her lie there miserably, and after a while Amanda's desperation began to gather into a sort of anger that he could be so obtuse. After all the joy they had shared, was one phone call really all it took to make him change his mind about her? If he'd loved her, he would have believed anything she said, and he certainly wouldn't have let her cry herself to sleep.

As a result, she treated Blair with stiff formality at breakfast the next day. He was looking decidedly dour, but Amanda was prepared to bet that *he* hadn't spent the night crying into his pillow. That only made her feel worse.

Breakfast itself was a fractious affair. Blair had agreed to take all the children to the airport to pick Belinda up, and they were consequently excited and inclined to be obstreperous, squabbling together about who was to sit where in the car, until he snapped at them, threatening to go on his own unless they all shut up.

'What about me?' said Amanda as the children scurried off to get ready, and Blair turned to bite *her* head off.

'I haven't got room for you as well as Belinda and all her stuff!'

'I wasn't talking about coming to the airport,' she said distantly. 'I was simply going to ask when you want me to go back to London. Once your sister is here, I presume you won't need me any more.'

Instead of sweeping her into his arms and assuring her that he would always need her, Blair only scowled. 'I can't discuss that now!' he said curtly. 'I'm late as it is, and if those bloody children don't hurry up I'll be even later. I'll talk to Belinda about the details when she gets back.'

Charming! After all they had shared, her departure was a mere 'detail' to be discussed with his sister! Left alone, Amanda slammed around the castle all day, lurching from fury to utter despair and back again. What would Belinda care about when she left? She would be packed off onto the first train south and that would be that!

But in the event it was Belinda who ensured that she stayed. Blair's sister was a fragile-looking blonde with a sweet face and big blue eyes that were much sharper than they looked, and they glanced as if casually from Blair to Amanda without appearing to notice the unspoken tension between them. When the children had been persuaded to bed after all the excitement, she made a point of looking for Amanda.

She found her in the kitchen, drearily washing up after supper. 'I wanted to thank you properly for looking after the children,' she said, picking up a teatowel. 'You've obviously done a marvellous job and they all think you're wonderful. It was Amanda this and Amanda that all the way back from the airport!'

'They've been wonderful too,' said Amanda with a catch in her voice. She couldn't bear to think about how much she would miss them.

'It was a stroke of luck for us that you were prepared to come for Christmas,' Belinda went on. 'It can't have been easy, being so far from your own family and friends, and you probably didn't bank on being snowed in with just Blair and the children for company.'

'No.' Amanda's throat was tight with unshed tears. She hadn't banked on falling in love with Blair either. There were a lot of things she hadn't banked on.

Unaware that Belinda was studying her averted profile, she stacked another plate on the draining-board. The other girl began to dry it. 'It might have been awkward if you and Blair hadn't got on so well together,' Belinda said casually. 'The kids seemed to think you and he were good friends.'

'Did they?' Amanda concentrated fiercely on washing up.

'Weren't you?'

She thought of the times when Blair had pulled her laughing down into his lap, the nights they had held each other close and talked. 'Sometimes,' she huskily.

'Funny, that's what Blair said too when I asked him if you got on,' said Belinda. 'He wasn't very forthcoming, though. When I asked him what you were like, he just said that I would have to judge for myself.' She grinned. 'Sometimes he can be the most exasperating man!'

'I know,' said Amanda with feeling, just as Blair came into the kitchen.

'Ah, Blair!' said Belinda innocently. 'We were just talking about you.'

The colour rushed into Amanda's face. 'Actually, I was just

about to ask Belinda when she would like me to go,' she said with an attempt at dignity.

'I see.' Blair looked grim.

Neither was aware of Belinda's perceptive glance from one to the other. 'Don't go just yet,' she said quickly. 'It was a hellish flight back, and I'm bound to be jet-lagged for a few days. You could stay a few more days, surely?' She looked appealingly at her brother. 'That would be all right, wouldn't it, Blair?'

'Of course,' he said stiffly after a moment's hesitation.

'Good, that's settled, then,' said Belinda with satisfaction. 'That is, you *will* stay, won't you, Amanda?'

Blair's reluctance had not been lost on Amanda. Half of her said that if she had any pride at all she would insist on leaving by the next train. The other half urged her to seize the chance to put things right with Blair. If she left now, she might never have the opportunity to explain why she had come to Dundinnie or how she had fallen in love with him. If she left now, she would have to say goodbye, and she didn't think she could bear to do that just yet.

'Yes, I'll stay,' she said.

Finding the right moment to confess to Blair was easier said than done. There was no sign of him at breakfast the next morning, and when Amanda asked where he was in a deliberately offhand manner Belinda could only roll her eyes.

'I saw him striding off into the distance from my bedroom window. He looked in a foul mood, so I wasn't tempted to follow him!' She glanced at Amanda. 'What's going on?'

'You'd better ask Blair,' snapped Amanda, frustrated at not being able to unburden herself of her guilt now that she had finally screwed up enough courage to confess.

'I have,' said Belinda. 'He wouldn't tell me either.'

Amanda decided it was time to change the subject. 'How's your jet lag?' she asked before Blair's sister could ask any more awkward questions. Belinda stared at her fixedly for a moment before obviously resigning herself to the fact that she might as well give up.

'I'm a bit disorientated still, but otherwise I feel fine.'

'You're lovely and brown. Did you have good weather?'

'Perfect. I had a marvellous time,' Belinda told her, sitting back in her chair and cradling a mug of coffee between her hands. 'It was a shame that Lynn had that accident, of course, but she wasn't badly hurt and I didn't mind helping her out with boring things like cooking and cleaning after she'd done so much for me. I was a mess when I arrived,' she confessed. 'Paul left me with the self-confidence of a gnat, and a pretty inadequate gnat at that, but I feel so different now. Being alone gave me a chance to think, and I realised that I married him for all the wrong reasons.'

She paused and smiled ruefully. 'When we first met, Paul reminded me of Malcolm, my cousin. They were both handsome and charming and they had the same sort of recklessness, but it's not easy living with a man who's completely unpredictable. Paul thrived on risk. He used to sneer at me because I always wanted to take the safe option, while I used to wish that he could be a completely different kind of husband—someone steady and kind who would look after me instead of treating me like an accessory.' She sighed. 'I suppose I'm not the first woman to make a fool of herself by believing that she could change a man just by marrying him! You've got to love them for what they are, not for what you'd like them to be.'

Amanda thought of Blair, who could be so dour and pigheaded, and yet so tender. His warmth and his stubbornness were part of the same man. It was no good loving one without the other. 'There's no point in expecting them to be perfect,' she agreed. 'Only that they're perfect for you.'

Belinda nodded, and it occurred to Amanda that she would like Iain Ferguson. He was strong and kind and had a reassuringly dependable air that would make any woman feel se-

cure. She ought to introduce them to each other, but if she
rang Iain and invited him to Dundinnie Blair would probably
misunderstand that too, and it would only make matters worse.

Amanda was still trying to work out a way of contacting
Iain that wouldn't immediately appear underhand when she
met him in the village shop that afternoon, and the matter
resolved itself. Blair had come back only to shut himself in
his study, and the boys were fighting about whose water-pistol
was whose, so Belinda and Emily voted to walk down to the
village with Amanda to visit Maggie while she bought some
fresh milk. After the thaw, the roadside was slushy and splattered with mud where the cars had passed. It looked as dreary
as Amanda felt.

Iain was tossing a selection of cans into a basket when she
spotted him wedged at the end of the narrow aisle. 'That
doesn't look very healthy,' she said, nodding down at his
shopping, and he spun round, his face lighting up when he
saw her.

'Amanda! Just what the doctor ordered!' He beamed down
at her. 'Don't tell me you've been snowbound all this time?'

'Until a couple of days ago.'

'How was your Christmas?'

Amanda thought of Christmas night—of the still, silent
night and the soaring passion that she and Blair had discovered
together. How could she ever explain to anyone what
Christmas had been like?

'It was...fine,' she said in the end.

She had forgotten how easy Iain was to talk to, and they
stood chatting for a few minutes before he asked her what
plans she had for that night. She looked at him blankly. 'Tonight?'

Iain eyed her with mock sympathy. 'You *have* been out of
it! Don't tell me you've forgotten the new year starts tomorrow? It's hogmanay—time to celebrate!'

What was there to celebrate when Blair had hardly spoken

to her for two days? Amanda summoned a smile. 'Blair's sister only got back from New Zealand yesterday and she'll probably still be jet-lagged. She won't want to stay up and see the new year in.'

'Who says?' said Belinda humorously from behind her. 'Maggie was just on her way out to see a friend, so we came on to find you,' she explained. 'Little did I think we'd find you rejecting the possibility of a social life!' She grinned at Amanda's consternation. 'Don't worry, I'm only teasing—but really, I feel fine.'

'Mummy, this is Iain.' Emily, hanging onto her mother's hand and gazing worshipfully at Iain, was bursting to introduce them and got in just as Amanda opened her mouth to do the same.

Iain and Belinda regarded each other with frank pleasure and Amanda watched the instant liking between them a touch wistfully. It was very different from her own first meeting with Blair. Why couldn't she have fallen in love with someone easygoing like Iain, who would never leave her feeling miserable and confused the way Blair did?

But then someone easygoing wouldn't make love to her the way Blair did. He wouldn't have Blair's hands or Blair's smile or Blair's ability to dissolve her bones with a single look.

'Amanda?'

Amanda snapped back to attention to find Belinda and Iain watching her with amusement. Already they looked as if they belonged together. 'You haven't been listening to a word, have you?' said Belinda, resigned.

'S-sorry,' stammered Amanda, terrified that the intensity of her feelings for Blair was stamped all over her face. 'I was miles away.'

'I've invited Iain to supper,' Belinda repeated patiently. 'Do you think we can make something from what's in the larder, or should we get something while we're here?'

Amanda forced herself to sound enthusiastic as Belinda discussed recipes. She was delighted that Belinda and Iain were getting on as well as she had thought they would, but she couldn't help wondering what Blair would think when he heard that Iain was coming to dinner, and how she could ensure that he knew it was Belinda who had invited him.

Fortunately, Belinda told him herself, but Amanda suspected that Blair blamed her anyway. He scowled when he heard who they were entertaining, but he had no choice but to offer Iain a drink when he arrived that night, and his initial dour suspicion faded slightly when it became obvious that the doctor was far more interested in his sister than in Amanda. Belinda, in fact, was on sparkling form and kept Iain by her side, effectively forcing Amanda and Blair together.

Amanda appreciated her motives, but the constraint between them made it impossible for Amanda to talk naturally to Blair and they ended up sitting tensely apart, the stiffness of their conversation in marked contrast to Belinda and Iain's laughter. When she thought of how they too had once delighted in each other, Amanda's throat tightened with tears.

The evening seemed interminable. In defiance of jet lag, Belinda was determined to keep them all up until midnight and Amanda could only marvel at her stamina while longing for an excuse to slip away. It was obvious that Iain would have been quite happy to be left alone with Belinda, and equally obvious that Blair was hating this as much as she was and couldn't wait to get away from her.

When midnight finally struck, they both pinned on false smiles and somehow got through the flurry of kisses and handshakes without managing to touch each other once. If they had hoped that neither of the others had noticed, however, they were doomed to disappointment. 'You two haven't wished each other a happy New Year,' said Belinda clearly, and something in her tone made Iain turn and look at Blair and Amanda with interest.

There was a pause. Amanda stood very still, swamped by

painful memories of how she and Blair had wished each other
a happy Christmas only a week ago. Then Blair had smiled
as he'd pulled her into his arms; now he just stood there rigidly
as if he couldn't bear to touch her. Her eyes stung with tears,
and she was turning to run out of the room, regardless of what
Belinda and Iain thought, when Blair reached out and caught
hold of her wrist.

'I was just about to,' he said woodenly, pulling her back
towards him. His face was quite impassive and, smarting with
humiliation, Amanda tried to tug her arm free, but his grip
only tightened. It was impossible to tell what he was thinking.
'Happy New Year, Amanda,' he said, and before she could
move he had bent his head and brushed her mouth with his.

It was the barest of kisses, but that one brief touch was
enough to unleash all the pent-up passion of the past two days.
The old magic jolting between them caught both unprepared
and their lips clung together as if they had a life of their own,
so that it was almost without thinking that Amanda melted
into Blair and opened her mouth to the questing excitement
of his tongue. With a sigh that might have been of release, he
let go of her wrist and lifted his hands to tangle his fingers in
her soft hair, and before either of them realised quite what had
happened they were kissing hungrily, almost frantically—
deep, urgent kisses that said more than words ever could.

Belinda and Iain were utterly forgotten. All that mattered
was to be able to hold each other again, and there was no need
for discussion or explanation as Blair took Amanda by the
hand and led her up the huge staircase to his room. Murmuring
incoherent endearments, fumbling in their haste, they undressed each other and fell at last into the big, wide bed where
they made love with a fierceness that left them awed and
shaken and gasping for breath.

Afterwards, when their breathing had returned to normal,
Amanda played her fingers over Blair's chest, loving the texture of his skin and suppleness of his body. 'Belinda must be

wondering what on earth's happened to us,' she said with a contented sigh, and Blair grinned.

'I'm sure she knows exactly what's happened,' he said, smoothing his own hand possessively down her spine and pretending to sound aggrieved. 'She set us up!'

Amanda snuggled against him. 'I'm glad she did.'

'So am I,' admitted Blair. 'I was furious with her at first for inviting that doctor friend of yours. I thought she was trying to throw you two together until I realised that she was doing her best to cut you out. I'm afraid you've lost an admirer there!'

'I know,' said Amanda with mock regret. 'It looks as if I'll just have to make do with you instead, doesn't it?' Shifting so that she could look down into Blair's face, she dropped a teasing kiss onto his lips. 'But I think I might survive!'

Blair caught her back to him as she made to lift her head and they exchanged a long, warm kiss. 'I'm sorry I've been such a brute, Amanda,' he said at last, drawing a ragged sigh and settling her into his shoulder so that he could hold her comfortably against the hard length of his body. 'I've been out of my mind with jealousy ever since I picked up the phone and heard that bloody friend of yours asking for you as if he owned you. He sounded so smooth, so sure of you that I wanted to reach down the phone and punch him, and then I found myself remembering everything you'd told me about your life in London.

'I remembered what you'd said about Hugh and how irritated you'd been at the idea of commitment, and suddenly...' He trailed off, running his fingers through her hair with a rueful smile, as if embarrassed by his own reaction. 'I don't know...suddenly it seemed as if that was your real life and this—being here with me—was just an interlude for you. And then you talked about going back to London and I realised that I didn't want you to go, and I was so angry with myself for falling in love with you when you didn't love me that I couldn't think straight. I didn't know what to do with myself until Bindie pushed me into kissing you and then it was all very clear and I realised that that was all I'd wanted to do all along.'

Amanda barely heard his last words. 'You're in love with me?' she whispered, starry-eyed, scarcely daring to believe it was true.

'Surely you knew that?' said Blair tenderly, rolling her beneath him once more.

She shook her head wordlessly. The hard weight of his body covering hers, the knowledge that he was there, that he loved her, that he didn't want her to go all threatened to overwhelm her, but joy was suffused with a lingering guilt. She still hadn't told him the truth about herself.

'Blair?' she said in a rush.

'Hmm?'

Amanda took a deep breath. 'I've got something to tell you,' she began, but Blair was distracting her by drifting his hand up the back of her thigh while he teased tiny kisses along her collar-bone. 'Blair,' she started again almost desperately, and he lifted his head reluctantly to smile down into her face.

'What?'

His eyes were so warm, his smile so tender, his touch so tantalising that Amanda felt desire wrench at her heart, quickening her breath and crumbling her resolve once more. She couldn't bear to spoil this moment. If she told him now, at the very best they would have to stop, to sit up and waste the night in arguments and explanations. At the worst, he would turn away and the flinty look would shutter his face. It would be like taking a hammer to the closeness between them.

'What is it?' said Blair again as she hesitated, and he smoothed her hair coaxingly behind her ears. 'Tell me.'

'I...I...' Amanda struggled against her conscience then succumbed to the longing that churned through her. 'I love you,' she burst out before she could say anything different, and once the words were out she couldn't stop. 'I love you, I love you, I love you,' she said desperately over and over again, pulling him down and covering his face with kisses. 'I love you; I do…I do…I *do*!'

Blair laughed shakily at her vehemence, but his eyes blazed with expression as he pinned her down, holding her arms out-stretched. 'Don't go back to London,' he said urgently, and Amanda looked up into his face and felt as if she would shatter with love.

'I'll stay as long as you want me.'

'You could be in for a very long stay,' warned Blair, releasing her arms so that he could gather her close once more, but Amanda only smiled.

'Good,' she said, and then his mouth came down on hers and everything else was forgotten.

CHAPTER TEN

'HAPPY New Year again!' Blair woke Amanda with a cup of tea and a kiss the next morning. He had drawn the curtains to reveal a perfect winter day, scintillating with cold and light, and she stretched luxuriously in the sunlight.

January the first—a new year, a new start. Never had a year beckoned with the promise of so much happiness. With Blair by her side, anything was possible. Amanda leant back against the pillows and they smiled wordlessly at each other as he sat down on the edge of the bed. Her eyes were golden in the sunshine and soft with memories of the night, but her expression was vivid with the exhilaration that danced along her veins, and Blair caught his breath as he leant forward to kiss her again.

He was barefoot and bare-chested, having clearly pulled on a pair of trousers simply to make the tea. 'Aren't you cold?' murmured Amanda, sliding her hands lovingly over the muscles in his arms, and he smiled wickedly as he tumbled her down with him into the bed.

'Cold? Not with you around!'

'You don't think we ought to get up?' she said provocatively, even as she began to unfasten his trousers.

'Get up?' he mumbled between kisses. 'What for?'

'Well...Belinda...and the children,' Amanda managed, breathless beneath the delicious onslaught of his hands.

'Belinda,' said Blair, 'has tactfully taken the kids off to spend the day with Iain, so you and I can stay in bed as long as we like—unless there's something you'd rather do, of course?'

169

'No,' she said with a sigh of contentment. 'I can't think of anything.'

They did get up in the end, of course, but it was early afternoon before Amanda sank into a deep bath, so relaxed and replete that she kept sliding down into the bubbles. Afterwards, light-headed with euphoria, she floated downstairs in a haze of happiness so complete that it took her a few minutes to register that the dream-like state that had enveloped her since Blair's lips had touched hers the night before had irrevocably shattered and that she was back in the nightmare.

'Sorry. Have I been ages?' said Amanda as she caught sight of Blair standing in the door of his study. 'I had such a wonderful bath,' she went on, dancing down the last stairs and not even noticing the rigid tension in his stance or the stony expression on his face. 'It was all I could do to—'

'Come in here.' Blair's voice cut her off like knife and he turned on his heel and disappeared into his study.

Puzzled, but still smiling, half expecting him to be teasing or about to surprise her, Amanda followed. Her smile faded when she went up to him and saw him flinch away rather than touch her. Only then did she realise that there was a white set look about his mouth and that his eyes were bleaker and more bitter than she had ever seen them.

Without a word, Blair walked over to his desk and handed her a cheque. Amanda stared at it uncomprehendingly. 'What's this?' she said slowly. She felt disorientated, as if she had been jerked out of a deep sleep, unsure what was dream and what was reality.

'Payment for services rendered.' Blair bit out the words.

She shook her head to clear it. 'I don't understand. What is this, Blair? What's going on?'

'You came up here to do a job, didn't you?'

'Yes,' said Amanda warily.

'You did a good job, too,' he went on, as if she hadn't spoken. A muscle was jumping frantically in his cheek and he was obviously struggling to keep an iron grip on his control. 'No one could say that you haven't been a good nanny, and we wouldn't want you to go back to London without any reward for your hard work, would we? Especially not when the agency are hardly likely to cough up when I tell them that the girl they sent never arrived and the one I got was most certainly not a nanny!'

Amanda went very still. 'How did you find out?' she asked dully.

'Your boss decided it was time he spoke to me himself,' said Blair in a glacial voice. 'He rang while you were in the bath.'

'Norris?'

'Yes, *Norris!*' he repeated savagely. 'How many other bosses do you have?'

'But he said he'd give me a week!' Amanda burst out before she could help herself, realising too late the effect of her words on Blair. He looked as if she had spat at him.

'So it's true?'

Amanda sank down into a chair and buried her face in her hands. '*Is* it?' he asked harshly again.

'It's true that I'm not a nanny,' she said, her voice muffled through her hands.

'And your name isn't Susan Amanda Haywood either, is it?'

'No.'

Blair moved stiffly round to sit behind his desk as if he wanted to keep as much distance between them as possible. 'Would you care to tell me where the real Susan Haywood has been all this time?'

'She went to California with her boyfriend,' said Amanda wearily. 'But none of this is her fault. I persuaded her to let me take her place. It was all my idea.'

'Oh, I can believe that!' jeered Blair. 'Was it all your idea to seduce me as well?'

'No!'

'So you were just following orders, in fact?'

'No!' she cried again, horrified at how quickly the sweetness of the night had shattered into bitterness and anger. 'It wasn't like that!'

'Wasn't it? Why is it, then, that Norris Jeffries is so familiar with the progress of our relationship? He seemed to know all about us.' Amanda dropped her head despairingly back into her hands, wanting only to shut out the hurt and betrayal she recognised in Blair's fury. 'When I told him just what he could do with his offer, he was more than ready to tell me all about you and how you've kept him informed about every move you've made since you've been here.'

She shook her head miserably. 'It's not true!'

'You mean you didn't tell Jeffries you were sleeping with me? You didn't tell him you'd got me prepared to do anything to keep you?'

Blair's words lashed at Amanda and desperate tears prickled her eyes. 'I just let him think that,' she tried to explain. 'I didn't want anything more to do with the project and I was afraid he'd contact you himself.'

'I'm sure you were! You couldn't have me knowing the truth, could you?'

'I was going to tell you,' she said, still struggling with tears. 'I tried to tell you last night, but I knew it would spoil everything…'

'Oh, yes!' snarled Blair. 'You'd never get me to agree to sell Dundinnie that way, would you? Much better to keep me in the dark and carry on lying! Jeffries said you were desperate to bring off the deal so that you could gain a foothold in his company. He said you were the sort of girl who'd do *anything* to get what she wanted, and it seems he was right.' He spread his hands on the desk and looked down at them as if to check that they weren't shaking. 'You let me fall in love with you,' he accused her. His voice was quieter, but it chilled Amanda to the bone. 'You let me believe you loved me too. God, when it comes to lying, you make Iona look like an amateur!'

'I do love you!' She had given up the unequal struggle and the tears were pouring down her cheeks. 'You know that's true!'

'No, I don't know!' Blair shouted, slamming his hand down on his desk so hard that Amanda flinched. Erupting from his chair, he strode round until he towered over her, thrusting his face down into hers until she cowered. 'That's the whole point, Amanda—I *don't* know. I don't even know your real name! You've lied from start to finish. You're not called Susan, you're not a nanny, you don't even have a great-great-grandmother who got eaten by cannibals, do you? Can you give me one good reason why I should believe that you love me when everything else has been a lie?'

'*Please*, Blair, you must listen to me—'

'No,' he said, clamping abruptly down on his seething temper. He straightened contemptuously and stepped away as if from a bad smell. 'No, I've done enough listening to your stories. I want you out of here before Belinda and the children get back. The children at least deserve to keep their innocence for a few more years, so I hope you won't make me have to explain to them how you've used us all for the sake of your precious promotion. We'll tell them that your agency rang with an emergency job, shall we?' he went on, making no attempt to disguise his sarcasm. 'And that you, being the dedicated, professional nanny that you are, responded to the call without delay. Or is that too straightforward a story for someone with your fantastic approach to the truth?'

'You want me to go?' said Amanda slowly, incredulously. Even after everything he had said, she couldn't accept that it could end like this.

'Got it in one,' said Blair brutally. 'You can have half an hour to pack, and then I'll take you to the bus stop. After that I never want to set eyes on you again.'

'So that's it?' Unable to face the pain just yet, Amanda concentrated on the anger that jostled with black despair in her heart. 'One phone call from Norris and you're prepared to believe *him* utterly.'

'You admitted yourself that what he told me was true.'

'But you won't even give me a chance to explain! Doesn't everything we've shared mean anything to you? Christmas, last night...do they mean nothing?'

'They didn't mean anything to you except a chance for promotion,' said Blair, his face cold and closed. 'I'm afraid you've blown that, though. Norris wasn't very pleased when he realised that even all your efforts in bed weren't enough to persuade me to sell. He told me to tell you that he's not interested in failures, so you needn't bother to go back to the office—but perhaps you'll be able to seduce your way back into favour with him. You've got plenty of experience, after all.'

Amanda stared at him. Every word of Blair's was a knife, twisting and wrenching until she felt quite dead and cold inside. She was still holding the cheque he had handed her what seemed like a lifetime ago, before all her hopes and her happiness had come crashing down around her. Blair wasn't going to listen to her, she realised dully, and all that mattered now was to fight her way through the black haze of misery and get herself out of the room before she splintered into a thousand jagged fragments of pain.

Very slowly, she tore the cheque into tiny pieces and dropped them on the floor, before turning like an old woman for the door. 'I'll get my things,' she said.

'Oh, Amanda, I'm so grateful to you!' Sue danced Amanda around the room, her new engagement ring winking in the light. 'Everything's worked out wonderfully! If you hadn't persuaded me to go to California with Nigel, we wouldn't be getting married. We really had a chance to talk while we were away, and now I'm so happy and it's all thanks to you! You were right as usual. You got what you wanted, Blair McAllister got the children looked after, and I got Nigel... What could be better?'

Amanda tried to apologise about the agency, who had written a vitriolic letter when they'd heard what had happened from Blair, but Sue brushed it aside. 'I was leaving anyway,' she said gaily. 'Nigel wants us to get married as soon as possible, and right now I don't care about anything else!'

Smiling mechanically, Amanda agreed that everything had worked out for the best. Fortunately Sue seemed too taken up with her wedding plans to notice the anguish in the sherry-brown eyes or the pain in Amanda's voice, and she didn't ask what Christmas had been like.

Amanda was glad of it. The thought of Dundinnie was a constant ache, and she knew that she couldn't talk about it without breaking down in tears. The journey back to London had been a nightmare. Both she and Blair had forgotten that there was no public transport in Scotland on January the first, and if a kindly couple driving to visit family in the nearest town hadn't taken pity on her where she stood abandoned at the bus stop, Amanda would have been there all night. As it was, she had to spend the night at the town's one modest hotel and take her chance with the patchy transport service the next day.

Not that she had really cared. Too miserable even to cry, she had been carried remorselessly further and further away from Dundinnie until she had ended up back at the flat she shared with three friends. Never had Amanda felt so desperate. Previously any obstacles had brought out her fighting spirit, and she had bounced back with even bigger and better plans than before. All that had changed. What was the point of making plans when plans wouldn't change Blair's mind?

It had been easy before. She had seen ahead only a short step at a time—a new job, a new project—but now her entire life stretched out before her, bleak and empty and utterly meaningless without Blair. Sue had once accused her of not knowing what she wanted; well, now she did. She wanted to be back at Dundinnie; she wanted to burrow into Blair's hard strength and let him shelter her from the world. She wanted to be able to reach out and touch him, taste him, feel him. She wanted to be able to wake in the morning and know that he was there.

But she couldn't have what she wanted and now nothing else mattered.

Amanda had never needed her courage more than now. She made a valiant attempt to pretend to friends that everything was normal and got herself a job as a temporary secretary that gave her far too much time to think. She would sit at the word processor while the traffic grumbled outside the window and fax machines oozed endless rolls of shiny paper and it would all slip out of focus and she could imagine that she was sitting in front of the fire at Dundinnie. The candles would be flickering on the Christmas tree, the snow would be swirling outside, shut out by the heavy red curtains, and the air would be warm with the scent of pine cones and the faint spice of cinnamon.

And sometimes, when the longing was very bad, she would let herself imagine that Blair was sitting beside her, that he was turning to her with that smile that dissolved her bones, that he was reaching for her, pulling her down onto the hearthrug, making love to her in the firelight.

Then a phone would ring and a door would bang, and Amanda would find herself staring blankly at the screen with slow tears trickling down her cheeks.

Four ghastly weeks passed until she let herself into the flat one evening as the phone rang. She heard one of her flatmates answer it, and then her name was called. 'Amanda, is that you? Phone for you.'

'Who is it?' she asked listlessly, dropping her coat onto a chair.

'Belinda something.'

Amanda's mouth dried, and when she picked up the receiver her hands were slippery. 'Hello.' It came out as little more than a croak.

'Amanda? It's Belinda here, from Dundinnie. How are you?'

'Fine.' Her throat was so tight that she could hardly speak. 'How did you find me?'

'I managed to get Susan Haywood's number out of the agency, and I persuaded her to give me *your* number. You don't mind, do you?'

'No, I...' Amanda swallowed. 'You know about me taking Sue's place, then?'

'I prised some of the story out of Blair eventually,' said Belinda, and Amanda felt her heart stop at the very sound of his name.

'I'm sorry,' she managed after a moment. 'I behaved very badly.'

'Nonsense,' said Belinda robustly. 'You were marvellous with the kids, and that's all that matters as far as I'm concerned.'

'How...how are they?'

'Oh, they're fine. Still missing you. In fact, it's about the children that I rang,' she explained. 'Iain and I are planning to get married, so we're all going to stay up here.'

'That's wonderful news,' said Amanda with genuine feeling. 'I always thought you'd be just right for each other.'

Belinda laughed happily. 'Well, we're both very grateful to you for introducing us! The thing is,' she went on, 'Iain's got a locum arranged for next week and we thought it would be a nice idea to have some time with just the two of us. We want to go to France, but the kids are all at local schools now and as it's not half-term or anything we really need someone to keep an eye on them. They're quite happy to stay…but only if you look after them.' She paused. 'You wouldn't consider it, would you, Amanda? It would mean so much to them.'

'What about…your brother?' Amanda asked through stiff lips, unable even to say his name. 'Wouldn't they rather be with him?'

'Blair's away,' said Belinda, a little too casually. 'He's doing the recce for some trip to Indonesia or something. So, you see, it has to be you! Do say you'll come!'

A vision of Dundinnie rose up before Amanda. It would ache with memories of Blair, but right now memories were the only contact with him she had. What could it hurt if he wasn't going to be there? And at least it would give her a chance to see the children and say goodbye properly. The temptation was too great to be resisted.

'All right,' she said. 'I'll come.'

'Wonderful!' said Belinda. 'Let me know which train you're on and we'll meet you at the station.'

Five days later, Amanda stepped off the train just as she had done before, only this time from a standard-class coach. The journey had been bitter-sweet with memories, and she had nearly convinced herself that it had been a mistake to come. How was she going to be able to bear Blair's absence? She knew that she would look for him everywhere, and every time she would hurt anew when he wasn't there. It would be a refined form of torture.

On the train, Amanda had decided that the only way to survive was to avoid the places that reminded her too painfully of Blair. It would be different this time. Belinda was meeting her and she would be staying at Iain's house. There would be nothing of Blair there.

Even so, as she stopped to pick up her bag, she couldn't help glancing along the platform to where Blair had stood and waited for her before. The Christmas banner had gone—just like all her hopes, thought Amanda sadly—but as her eyes moved down to the empty space where Blair had once been she froze and the air whooshed from her lungs.

A man was standing there. A man with Blair's lean strength and Blair's dark features. A man scanning the crowd with Blair's penetrating eyes which held an anxious expression that wasn't Blair's at all. As she stared, still crouched over her bag, his urgently searching gaze met hers through the press of passengers moving towards the exit and jolted to a stop.

Trembling, Amanda straightened very slowly. Blair was in Indonesia. He never wanted to see her again. It couldn't be Blair.

Could it?

She squeezed her eyes closed, bracing herself against the bitter disappointment of realising that it was no more than a mirage, an impossible dream conjured up by the force of her longing, but when she opened them again he was still there, still staring at her through the shifting crowd as if he too hardly dared to believe what he was seeing.

He took an uncertain step towards her, and then another, and then another, until he was shouldering his way hastily between the people without taking his eyes off her. Struggling against a great rolling, tumbling wave of shock, confusion, disbelief, hope, longing and, above all, the sheer joy of just seeing him again, Amanda could only stand, oblivious to the train behind her, to the crowds, to anything other than the man pushing towards her, while her heart cartwheeled crazily and her pulse boomed and thudded in her ears.

When he was about six feet away, she managed a hesitant step forward, only to stop as she lost her nerve. What if he was angry? What if he told her to get right back on the train? What if—?

'Amanda?' Blair halted just beyond arm's reach, and something in his stance relaxed, as if until then he had been expecting her to disappear. 'Amanda,' he said again on a sigh of relief.

Only then did Amanda allow herself to believe that it was really him. 'Blair,' she whispered, and then they just looked at each other.

It was *him*. It was really him. She drank in the sight of him. Every line, every angle of his face was just as she had remembered in the long, lonely nights since they had parted. His brows were still dark and fierce, his mouth was still set in the same heart-clenching line. Only his eyes were different. They held an uncertain, questioning expression that Amanda had never seen before.

Around them, whistles blew and doors slammed, announcements crackled incomprehensibly over the loudspeakers and train brakes hissed, but Blair and Amanda were aware of none of it. They stood facing each other, as if poised on the edge of something momentous, marooned together in a silence that strummed with unspoken dreams and memories.

The need to reach out and touch him was so strong that Amanda had to twist her hands together to stop them stretching out of their own accord. The force of Blair's personality tugged at her like a powerful magnet, and it was all she could do not to let herself be drawn inexorably towards him. Struggling to keep control of herself, she spoke first. 'I...I thought you were in Indonesia,' she said huskily.

'I was,' said Blair. 'I got home a week ago. I couldn't bear it any more.'

For Amanda it was almost enough to hear his voice. She didn't care what he said, as long as he kept on talking, kept on standing there where she could see him. 'Couldn't bear what any more?' she asked to make him speak again.

'Not having you there,' he answered simply, then paused, searching for a better way to explain. 'I flew out the day after I left you at that bus stop. I was so angry I just wanted to forget everything and I thought it would be easier where there were no memories of you to remind me. But it didn't make any difference, Amanda.'

He lifted his hands in a gesture of hopelessness and a rueful smile lifted the corners of his mouth. 'I couldn't get over the conviction that if I turned round you'd be there, smiling at me. I'd tell myself that it was impossible, that of course you couldn't be in Indonesia and even that I wouldn't want to see you anyway, but every time I'd turn and every time I was devastated to find that you weren't there.

'You were with me wherever I went, Amanda,' he went on, his voice deep and reverberating with memories. 'Wherever I went, whatever I did, you were there. I couldn't forget the feel of your skin or the scent of your hair or the way you smiled when you were teasing me. I tried, but it was as if you'd become a part of me, and it didn't take me long to realise that I didn't even want to try any longer. All I had to do was accept the truth—that I love you, I want you and I need you, and there's absolutely nothing that I can do about it.'

It had to be a dream. Amanda had listened, half-afraid to take in what Blair was saying. 'But I *lied* to you,' she said, her eyes shimmering with tears.

'Did you lie about loving me?'

She shook her head. 'No, never that.'

'Then that's all that matters, isn't it?' said Blair softly and held out his arms.

Still scarcely daring to believe that it was real, Amanda took a hesitant step forward. 'Do you really love me?' she whispered incredulously, and at last he smiled.

'I really do,' he said, reaching for her. 'And if you'll only say you'll marry me I'll spend the rest of my life showing you how much.'

'In that case I'll definitely marry you!' Amanda's smile was tremulous through her tears as, jubilant and relieved, Blair pulled her hard against him.

'You will?'

'I will, I will!' Half laughing, half weeping, Amanda flung her arms around his neck, and then his mouth came down on hers and the black misery of the last few weeks was swept away in the glorious, giddy relief of being able to hold each other again. They kissed—deep, hungry kisses—until they were breathless and then they kissed some more, unable to touch and taste and feel each other enough.

'Oh, Blair, I'm so sorry about everything,' mumbled Amanda eventually between kisses to his ear and his jaw. 'It was all my fault.'

'No, I'm the one who's sorry.' Blair smoothed the hair away from her cheeks and held her face between his hands so that he could look down into her eyes. 'I should have listened to you,' he said seriously. 'I should have trusted you and believed in you. It was just…such a shock. Iona taught me to hate deception of any kind and when you admitted lying it seemed to make a mockery of everything that we'd shared. It was only when I'd had time to think that I knew that what we'd had together was so special that it had to have been real. It was, wasn't it?'

'Yes, it was,' said Amanda. 'It still is,' she added, and kissed him again.

A station buggy tooting at them as it went past broke them apart at last and they laughed a little shakily. 'I suppose we'd better get out of here,' said Blair, registering for the first time the surreptitious but intensely interested stares of the passengers who had gathered to wait for the next train. He picked up her bag and, putting his other arm around her, led her out to the car.

Amanda patted it affectionately as he threw the bag into the back. 'Good old car! Perhaps we'll break down again and I'll be able to show you how much I've changed by holding the torch properly and not complaining about only having gingernuts to eat.'

'I don't want you to change,' Blair said, taking her by the

waist and pinning her against the car so that he could press tantalising kisses along the line of her jaw. 'I want you just the way you've always been—funny and warm and utterly exasperating,' he teased, and then his voice changed. 'And so desirable,' he finished as their lips met again in a long, blissful kiss.

'I love you...I love you...I love you,' said Amanda unsteadily after a while, kissing him almost desperately between the words.

'Amanda—' Blair gave a deep, satisfied sigh and rested his cheek against her hair '—I've missed you so much, I can hardly believe I'm holding you again. Nothing was the same without you. I came back to Dundinnie, thinking it was the closest I could get to you, and it was even worse than before. You were everywhere. I couldn't even get in the car without remembering that first time we met. I knew then that I had to get you back, but I didn't know how.'

'Surely you knew I'd have walked backwards around the world to be with you?' said Amanda, nestling happily into his arms.

She could feel Blair shake his head against her hair as he tightened his hold on her. 'I'd treated you so badly that you would have had every right to refuse to listen to me. I just hung onto the hope that if I could get you back up here everything would be all right.'

'So it was you who tracked me down, not Belinda?'

'That's right. I had to soothe all the ruffled feathers at the agency before they let me have Susan's number.'

'You spoke to Sue?' Amanda straightened abruptly. 'She never said anything to me!'

'I asked her not to,' Blair confessed. 'I was afraid you might not come back, but I did get some satisfaction from hearing that all your friends were worried about how miserable you were. After that, all I had to do was get Belinda to ring you.'

'Then all that about looking after the children was just an excuse? Aren't they getting married after all?'

'Oh, they're getting married all right,' he said. 'They're just not going away next week—at least I sincerely hope they're not! Much as I liked having the kids around, I want you to myself for a while.'

Amanda smiled contentedly and rested her head back on his shoulder. 'I hope you're being nicer to Iain now.'

'Since I've stopped wanting to tear his head from his shoulders every time he looked at you, I have to admit that he's immensely likeable.' Blair grinned. 'He's perfect for Bindie too.'

'Emily must be thrilled. She always thought Iain was wonderful.'

'Emily is very happy,' he agreed. 'So are the boys, now that they've got to know Iain, and Bindie is happiest of all!'

'She can't possibly be as happy as I am,' said Amanda, and Blair kissed her once more before opening the passenger door.

'Come on,' he said. 'Let's go home.'

Amanda watched Blair light the last candle on the tree and felt her heart contract with love. They had been married nearly a year, but desire could still catch her unawares. Sometimes all he had to do was turn his head or stretch his arm above his head, like now, and the breath would dry in her throat.

'What are you smiling at?' teased Blair, turning unexpectedly and catching his wife's shining look. She seemed to glow with happiness and he reached for her instinctively, tossing aside the box of matches so that he could pull her into the shelter of his arms.

'I was just thinking how much has changed since this time last year,' Amanda said contentedly.

'It's been quite a year, hasn't it?'

Now that he had Amanda, Blair had given up his travels, although he still acted as a consultant. Instead they had worked hard on plans to develop the estate and ensure that Dundinnie remained a home. Belinda and Iain were married and the children were well settled into their new life, although they still loved to stay at Dundinnie with Blair and Amanda.

They had clamoured to come over for Christmas Day, and Amanda was confident that she was as ready as she would ever be. The turkey was in the fridge, the mince pies ready to be warmed and dusted with icing sugar and the baubles on the tree winked and glimmered in the candlelight. Now all they had to do was sit back and enjoy the prospect of a long lie-in on Christmas morning.

'Remember how we sat here last year filling their stockings?' she said.

'All I remember is wanting to kiss you,' said Blair.

'It was fun, though, wasn't it? Christmas is always quiet without children.'

He kissed the lobe of her ear and ran a hand suggestively down her spine. 'I don't mind a quiet Christmas if it means I can be alone with you.'

A secret smile curled Amanda's mouth. 'You'd better make the most of this one, then,' she said demurely. 'You won't be having any more quiet Christmases for a few years to come.'

It took Blair a little time to register. When he did, he stiffened incredulously and held her away from him so that he could stare down at her. 'Amanda? You don't mean...?'

'Well, we did decide it was time we started to fill up some of the extra rooms,' she said, laughing up at his stunned expression.

'A *baby*...' A smile of astonished delight started in Blair's eyes and then spread over his face as what she'd said sank in. 'I know we talked about it but...I can't believe it! You've having a baby! *Our* baby.' Gathering Amanda back into his arms, he touched her all over as if she was infinitely precious. 'That's the best Christmas present you could ever have given me!'

'It's a present we've given each other,' said Amanda softly. 'A present we'll share.'

On the mantelpiece, the carriage clock began to strike twelve. 'Happy Christmas,' she said, safe and secure for ever in his arms, and Blair bent his head for a kiss that promised years of joy to come.

'Happy Christmas, darling!' he said.

If you enjoyed what you just read,
then we've got an offer you can't resist!

Take 2 bestselling
love stories FREE!
Plus get a FREE surprise gift!

Clip this page and mail it to Harlequin Reader Service®

IN U.S.A.	**IN CANADA**
3010 Walden Ave.	P.O. Box 609
P.O. Box 1867	Fort Erie, Ontario
Buffalo, N.Y. 14240-1867	L2A 5X3

YES! Please send me 2 free Harlequin Romance® novels and my free surprise gift. Then send me 4 brand-new novels every month, which I will receive months before they're available in stores. In the U.S.A., bill me at the bargain price of $2.90 plus 25¢ delivery per book and applicable sales tax, if any*. In Canada, bill me at the bargain price of $3.34 plus 25¢ delivery per book and applicable taxes**. That's the complete price and a savings of over 10% off the cover prices—what a great deal! I understand that accepting the 2 free books and gift places me under no obligation ever to buy any books. I can always return a shipment and cancel at any time. Even if I never buy another book from Harlequin, the 2 free books and gift are mine to keep forever. So why not take us up on our invitation. You'll be glad you did!

116 HEN CNEP

316 HEN CNEQ

Name	(PLEASE PRINT)	
Address	Apt.#	
City	State/Prov.	Zip/Postal Code

* Terms and prices subject to change without notice. Sales tax applicable in N.Y.
** Canadian residents will be charged applicable provincial taxes and GST.
   All orders subject to approval. Offer limited to one per household.
   ® are registered trademarks of Harlequin Enterprises Limited.

HROM99   ©1998 Harlequin Enterprises Limited

EXTRA! EXTRA!

The book all your favorite authors are raving about is finally here!

The 1999 Harlequin and Silhouette coupon book.

Each page is alive with savings that can't be beat!

Getting this incredible coupon book is as easy as 1, 2, 3.

1. During the months of November and December 1999 buy any 2 Harlequin or Silhouette books.

2. Send us your name, address and 2 proofs of purchase (cash receipt) to the address below.

3. Harlequin will send you a coupon book worth $10.00 off future purchases of Harlequin or Silhouette books in 2000.

Send us 3 cash register receipts as proofs of purchase and we will send you 2 coupon books worth a total saving of $20.00 (limit of 2 coupon books per customer).

Saving money has never been this easy.

Please allow 4-6 weeks for delivery. Offer expires December 31, 1999.

I accept your offer! Please send me (a) coupon booklet(s):

Name: _____

Address: _____ City: _____

State/Prov.: _____ Zip/Postal Code: _____

Send your name and address, along with your cash register receipts as proofs of purchase, to:

In the U.S.: Harlequin Books, P.O. Box 9057, Buffalo, N.Y. 14269
In Canada: Harlequin Books, P.O. Box 622, Fort Erie, Ontario L2A 5X3

Order your books and accept this coupon offer through our web site
http://www.romance.net
Valid in U.S. and Canada only.

PHQ4994R